# MURDER
# ON MIKE

A HARRY MacNEIL MYSTERY

# MURDER ON MIKE

BY H. PAUL JEFFERS

A
Joan
Kahn
BOOK

ST. MARTIN'S PRESS   NEW YORK

Copy editor: Harvey-Jane Kowa!

Library of Congress Cataloging in Publication Data

Jeffers, H. Paul (Harry Paul), 1934–
      Murder on mike.

      "A Joan Kahn book."

      I. Title.
PS3560.E36M84   1984      813'.54      84-16028
ISBN 0-312-55316-1

First Edition

10 9 8 7 6 5 4 3 2 1

*For Mike Ludlum*

"The weed of crime bears bitter fruit."
—*The Shadow*

# MURDER ON MIKE

## 1

The angelic face and the curvy figure belonged to Maggie Skeffington, but the voice—ah, the voice!—belonged to Miss Molloy, the sugary-throated but sharp-witted Gal Friday to the keenest pair of detectives on radio, Lieutenant Fitzroy and Sergeant O'Donnell of the Homicide Squad, who solved the most baffling murder cases Sunday nights on *Detective Fitzroy's Casebook* on the Blue Network. The thing I'd discovered about voices on the radio was that they hardly ever matched the faces of the actors. I'd hear a familiar voice in one of the saloons across Sixth Avenue from Radio City or along Swing Street only to turn around and discover that the deep and mellifluous baritone of an announcer I'd always pictured as another Clark Gable was really booming from the pipes of a guy who looked a lot more like Lou Costello or Mayor La Guardia. To this rule that people on the radio never look the way they sound, Maggie Skeffington was the exception. She actually had the Jean Harlow spun-gold hair, Rita Hayworth mouth, and Lana Turner figure that I endowed her with whenever I heard Miss Molloy encourage Fitzroy not to give up on the week's puzzler with the words that were Miss Molloy's trademark, "Gee, boss, this case is a tough one but I know you'll crack it." Or something to that effect.

There may have been someone who had not heard of *Detective Fitzroy's Casebook* a week before Maggie Skeffington walked into my office three flights up from the Onyx Club on Fifty-second Street, but by the time she parked herself nervously in front of my desk there couldn't've been anyone in New York who didn't know about the murder at Radio City. The finding of the body of radio's most popular detective in a studio with a bullet in his head had grabbed and held onto the headlines in the tabloids and given the gossip columnists a week of field days. The police had arrested the program's announcer for the murder.

"I don't care what the police say," asserted Maggie Skeffington with the plucky never-give-up Jean Arthur optimism that was also a staple of Miss Molloy, "David Reed did not kill Derek Worthington."

"How do you know he didn't?"

"David is not capable of murder."

"Everybody's capable of murder."

"David says he didn't do it and I believe him."

"Miss Skeffington, this isn't a radio broadcast. This is real life, a real murder. Take it from a man who knows about real-life crime, Sing Sing and Dannemora prisons are filled with guys who insist they didn't do it. I have yet to meet a chump doing time who didn't claim it was all a terrible miscarriage of justice. Naturally David Reed will deny he committed murder."

"Nonetheless, I believe him."

"Why?"

"A woman's intuition?"

I had to smile. A line like that would never have slipped from the lips of Miss Molloy; not in a month of Sundays. Miss Molloy was anything but naïve. "You've been acting in mystery programs long enough to know, Miss Skeffington, that even on the radio murder requires three elements: motive, means, and opportunity. From what I've read about the Worthington murder in the papers, Reed had all three. The cops have a pretty good case. From what I know of the New York Police Department, they don't go around arresting people for murder without having pretty compelling reasons. The cops didn't when I was in the department and I don't think they've started doing so since then. This case looks open and shut to me."

"I was led to believe that you were the man to see to get to the bottom of supposedly open-and-shut cases."

"Who told you that?"

"There was a newspaperman who came to the studios to report on the murder. A Mr. Ben Turner. When he interviewed me I told him that David was innocent. I took advantage of the opportunity to ask him, a crime reporter, how to go about hiring a private detective. He mentioned you."

"You were that certain that Reed didn't do it?"

"I was then and I am now."

"Excuse me for being direct, but are you and Reed what the gossip columns would call an item?"

"I love David, yes."

"Love is blind, Miss Skeffington."

"I assure you, Mr. MacNeil, that it's not blind love that brings me to you. David is just not the kind of person who would harm anyone. He's the kindest, most considerate, gentlest man I have ever known. Ask anyone who knows him. Cold-blooded murder is beyond his capabilities."

"Yet the police have charged him with shooting Derek Worthington to death. There'd been some trouble between them, if I remember correctly."

"Everyone had trouble with Derek."

"But did everyone threaten to kill him?"

"David didn't mean that. It was just one of those

−3−

things that people say in the heat of an argument."

" 'Someday I just may kill you.' I believe those are the exact words that Reed used."

"What of it? I said practically the same thing to Derek myself. Everyone in the cast has said it at one time or another. Derek was a man who provoked that kind of reaction from others."

"But of all those who might have had a reason to kill Derek Worthington, David Reed was the only one without an ironclad alibi for the time when Worthington was shot."

"You are up on the case, Mr. MacNeil."

"I paid it some attention. Crime is my business. And my hobby. Plus it was on the front pages all week. I appreciate your loyalty to Reed, Miss Skeffington, but—"

"Obviously Mr. Turner was wrong."

"I can't take your money and raise false hopes. Let it go, Miss Skeffington. Resign yourself to the fact that he did it. The evidence is there. He's bound to be indicted. Right now it's not a private investigator that Reed needs. Get him a good lawyer. I can recommend several if—"

"Thank you, Mr. MacNeil. I'm sorry to have taken your time."

She looked disappointed as she rose from the battered straight-backed chair in front of my matching secondhand oak desk, but by the time she reached the door and opened it, turning to look back at me as I cocked back in my creaking chair with my feet propped on the corner of the desk, she had a look in her blue eyes that showed me where Miss Molloy got that plucky never-give-up style that came through the radio. Looking at her in that instant I saw that Maggie Skeffington and Miss Molloy weren't two different people, one real and one imaginary, but the same gal. "What are you going to do now?" I asked.

She stuck out her pretty jaw. "Find another private eye."

"Wait a minute, Miss Skeffington."

"I'm not giving up on this, Mr. MacNeil. If you're not interested in the case, I'll find someone who is."

"Do you know what'll happen? Oh, you'll find another detective, but one without my scruples. He'll take your dough, string you along, keep you dangling while he piles up the expenses, and then *he'll* tell you that it's hopeless. Private detectives are a pretty sleazy bunch, you know." I stood up and smiled across my office at her. "Except me."

"However, you've turned me down."

"I've decided to change my mind and look into this case."

"Why?"

"Maybe I'm just a sucker for a sweet face."

"Mr. MacNeil, I doubt that you're a sucker for anything."

"Then let's just say that I don't want to see the gal who plays Miss Molloy hurt, which is exactly what will happen if anybody but me takes you on as a client. Where can I reach you to make my reports?"

"I'm at the Bristol on West Forty-eighth." I knew the hotel as one of those respectable inns where young women coming to New York in pursuit of their dreams of stardom on Broadway or the radio could live comfortably and safely until they made it or their money ran out. "About your fee." She opened a black patent leather purse.

"I usually get fifty dollars a day plus expenses," I said, taking the purse and snapping it shut. "I'll send a bill."

"How do you know I'm a person who'll pay you?"

I gave her back her purse. "If it turns out that David Reed is guilty, you'll have paid quite enough. If I turn up something that proves the guy is innocent, I'll collect my wages from him."

She looked at me teary-eyed. "Mr. Turner said you

were quite a guy." She smiled through the tears. "Actually he said something wonderful about you. He said, 'Harry MacNeil is the help of the hopeless.'"

"Would a newspaperman lie?"

## 2

Back in the days when Damon Runyon was cock of the roost and writing about the guys and dolls of Broadway and I was still a member of the New York Police Department, Runyon used to grab me by the arm, usually on his way into or out of Lindy's, and exclaim, "MacNeil, listen to the roar!" He meant the roar of New York; that is, Manhattan. When Runyon spoke of New York he always meant Manhattan. For me, Manhattan was best when the roar was muted down to a steady hum, which was the closest the big town ever got to silence. Between the time when the last jazz joint closed for the night and people who slept nights got up to go to work, the town whispered between a neon night reluctant to let go and a dawn hesitant about rousing the sun that would wake up Runyon's roar. Those wee hours of cracking dawn were crammed with surprises—a guy in a tuxedo strolling with a doll in an evening dress and bumping into a sleepy-eyed milkman rattling down the stoop of a brownstone, a Broadway dandy reeling from drink and coming face-to-face with a bakery boy dropping off bagels at a delicatessen smelling richly of perking coffee, a beat cop whistling a lonely tune down skyscraper canyons whose slick streets glistened after water wagons flooded the blacktop to wash the previous day's debris into sewers. Then you knew you couldn't live anywhere else, that no town on earth mattered as much to you as Manhattan, whether you happened to be the tuxedoed rich guy with the Broadway baby on your arm, a deliveryman, Damon Runyon, the whistling cop, or a middle-aged Irish private detective by the name of Harry Mac-Neil.

Once upon a time I'd been a cop. Up through the time when Jimmy Walker was mayor. Then I quit the force and went private for reasons my friends always wondered about but which I never explained. The reasons were good. It wasn't because I'd been on the take, as so many were at that time, because I never took anything when I was a cop. I didn't hand in my badge because I was afraid somebody would come around one day and ask for it. I just handed it in for reasons of my own and turned private. I was never put into one of his stories by Runyon, although he told me once that he'd thought about immortalizing me in print. "You are a character," he laughed, "but the trouble with you, Mac-Neil, is you're not a cartoon character like Harry the Horse or Nick the Greek or Johnny Broderick. Your curse, MacNeil, is that you're too damned straight." I got a good chuckle out of that.

Runyon had been the prince of the Broadway crowd in what he liked to call the gold rush, a time others would name the Roaring Twenties, the Jazz Age, the Flapper Era. Those gossamer days were already faded into legend by the time I became a private investigator, just before the country snapped to its senses and voted in Repeal, although the damage had been done: Prohibition had turned gangsters into millionaires who were not about to go out of business just because they couldn't bootleg hooch anymore. When I was putting away my policeman's uniform for a private eye's blue serge suit, the glitter of the gold rush had faded to the dull gray of the Depression. Those days, you could find a Runyon-esque character on nearly every corner selling apples.

A lot of my friends warned me that turning private investigator during the hard times would prove grim, yet all through the Thirties I'd worked and been fairly well paid and never once regretted handing in my gold detective's shield. In an unlucky country I was a lucky guy—lucky to be earning a living, lucky to be my own boss, lucky to be in New York.

If somebody wanted me or needed to hire me, I was in the book. Or he could ask anybody at the Onyx Club or Lindy's or any of the night spots in midtown. In most of the jazz joints along Fifty-second everybody knew the Mick dick.

It was, I believe, a jazz musician who first used the term the Big Apple to refer to New York, but it could have been anyone who understood that if you were going to make it in anything, the only place to make it where it really mattered was New York. That was true in jazz music. It was true in the theater. It was true for mobsters like Lucky Luciano, who still ran the rackets from his cell in Dannemora after D.A. Tom Dewey sent Charlie Lucky there on a white-slavery rap. It was true for the ink-stained wretches of the newspaper world such as Runyon, Walter Winchell, Leonard Lyons, Mark Hellinger, Ed Sullivan, and my pal Ben Turner, the best police reporter ever. And it was true for people like David Reed, Derek Worthington, and Maggie Skeffington, for whom New York was Radio City.

Most of the tourists and a lot of New Yorkers thought that all of Rockefeller Center was Radio City, but the name actually applied only to one part of the elegant complex of skyscrapers that old John D. Rockefeller had the gumption to build during the depths of the Depression, despite the common wisdom that the buildings could turn into real estate white elephants. When the Radio Corporation of America moved into the tallest of the buildings and gave the skyscraper its name, the company installed its radio stations, WEAF and WJZ, there and also two radio networks, the Blue and the Red, all of these broadcasting operations occupying the western end of the RCA Building under the name Radio City. That the huge theater on the opposite corner was named Radio City Music Hall contributed a good deal to everyone's misapprehension that all of John D.'s midtown enterprise was Radio City, but no matter what the people called the buildings poking skyward around a sunken plaza with its gleaming golden statue of Prometheus, Rockefeller Center immediately became the jewel of the Big Apple and a magnet for tourists along with the Empire State Building, the Statue of Liberty, the Chrysler Tower, and Times Square.

At the time when Maggie Skeffington came to see me about the murder of Derek Worthington just before Christmas 1939, New York was aglow not only with the seasonal decorations in Rockefeller Center and in the department stores along Fifth Avenue and at Herald Square, but also with the smashing success of the World's Fair, which had opened at Flushing Meadow. Reminders of the fair were everywhere. Store windows, restaurants, and advertising billboards boasted about the extravaganza just a quick subway ride from Rockefeller Center.

The fair and the attractions of Rockefeller Center were just what New York needed after a decade of gloomy Depression. Already the newspapers were filled with ads for hotels, clubs, and restaurants that were preparing for a gala evening to bid good-bye to the 1930s and to ring in the Forties with New Year's Eve festivities that a reveler could book for anywhere from $2.50 at the swinging Famous Door on Fifty-second Street to the $15-a-head fox-trot elegance of the Rainbow Room atop the RCA Building or the stately Waldorf-Astoria on ritzy Park Avenue.

The rebound was also evident on the Great White Way. Broadway was booming with one of the best seasons in memory, whether your taste ran to the zany with Olsen and Johnson in their smash-hit *Hellzapoppin* or to the gritty reality of the long-running *Tobacco Road* at the Forrest. If you wanted a message, there was *Key Largo* with Paul Muni at the Barrymore. If the classics were your speed, Maurice Evans was emoting at the Forty-fourth Street Theater in *Hamlet*. For lighter entertainment there were *Morning's at Seven* at the Longacre, *The Time of Your Life* at the Booth, *The Man Who Came to Dinner*'s outrageously funny takeoff on Alexander Woollcott at the Music Box, and *Life With Father* at the Empire. For evenings with a couple of women who could carry a show entirely on their own, theatergoers had Helen Hayes in *Ladies and Gentlemen* at the Martin Beck and Tallulah Bankhead in *The Little Foxes* at the National. There was also a lady with brass for a voice, Ethel Merman, belting out Cole Porter tunes in *DuBarry Was a Lady* and sharing the stage with Bert Lahr and leggy Betty Grable at the Forty-sixth Street Theater.

If you preferred movies, the blockbuster everyone had been waiting for, Margaret Mitchell's *Gone With the Wind*, had just tied Broadway traffic into knots with a double world premiere at the Capitol and Astor theaters.

You could taste the zesty optimism of a city and a country turning a corner of history just strolling around town. Certainly you could sense the rebound in the jazz clubs of Swing Street, that garish, noisy, bubbling block of former speakeasies between Fifth and Sixth avenues on Fifty-second. There, at number sixty-two, the Onyx, most nights, you could find me at the bar or in my office three flights up.

Sooner or later in the hours when the town was shifting from roar to hum, Ben Turner could be counted on to amble into the Onyx, the *Daily News* having been put to bed, its big boxy trucks bouncing all over town to deliver its daily chronicle in glaring headlines, big black-and-white photos, and snappy stories of the follies of the citizens of New York. The musicians were always in high gear by that time and in the mood to jam with anyone who could hold his own. That included me from time to time. I was pretty good with a clarinet and had even been told by some of the greatest jazzmen around that it was too bad I'd wasted my time being a cop instead of going for a career as a musician. Flattering as that was and as capable as I was sitting in with the bands, I never came up to their standards, not by a long shot.

I had just surrendered the clarinet to a pro and taken my customary perch at the corner of the Onyx bar just inside the front door when Ben Turner sauntered in, the Radio City murder case and Maggie Skeffington on his mind. I'd known this short, bald, bulb-nosed, ballsy, and bespectacled Jewish inhabitant of the Press Shack across from police headquarters on Centre Street since I was a beat cop and he was a cub reporter. I could read his face as easily as the front page of his tabloid and he knew it. Plopping down on the barstool next to me, he cocked back his snap-brim Adams hat and said, "I assume you let Miss Skeffington down easily."

"I took the case."

Ben looked askance at the jazz band in the rear of the club. Turning back to me, he said, "Excuse me, it must be the loud music, but I thought I heard you say you took the case."

"You heard right."

"Shit, Harry, I sent that gal to you because I figured you'd explain the facts of life to her. That Reed guy is guilty. Open and shut. You haven't fallen for that dame, I hope?"

"Well," I said, sipping a Scotch, "I'm not involved in a case at the moment, so what harm would it do to poke around this one a little?"

"You've got nothing to do? Why not just butt your

head against a wall? Seems to me it would be just as productive."

The bartender, an affable guy named Louie who'd been at the Onyx in all its incarnations at different addresses on Swing Street, brought Ben a Knickerbocker beer. He sipped it and wiped away a moustache of white foam as I explained why I took Maggie Skeffington on as a client. "Reed is guilty, probably, from what I've read in your newspaper, but this gal doesn't believe a word of it. If I look around a little, have a talk with the cops and the district attorney, check out some of the others who knew Derek Worthington and David Reed, I can come back to Miss Skeffington and lay it all out for her. Maybe I'll stand some chance then of getting her to accept the facts. She was going to scrounge up some other private dick, and you know what that would get her. Besides, it's the Christmas season, Ben. Goodwill to men."

"Not to mention misty-eyed dames," Ben grunted.

"Now that I've taken the case, I'm counting on you to fill me in. Who's in charge of the case at Homicide?"

"Your old pal Bill Tinney."

"And the district attorney?"

"Tim Brogan. They were both at the scene of the crime, of course, Bill doing his usual first-rate job of picking up the physical evidence. Brogan was going on his instincts. When the evidence and the instincts meshed, David Reed found himself sporting handcuffs."

"As quick as that?"

"Quick as that."

"Why all the hurry to make an arrest, I wonder?"

"Well, there was quite a pack of us newshounds in the hallway outside that studio. You know how newspaper guys are. There's nothing like a juicy murder involving celebrities and the glamour businesses like movies and radio to bring us swarming like a school of sharks smelling blood in the water. We were kept at a distance, but there was just too good an opportunity for some publicity, so Brogan and Tinney came out for a little press conference."

"Is Brogan running for something?"

"He will be in two years."

"I wish he weren't such a publicity hound."

"You didn't exactly shun the spotlight, Harry. You used to like to be on the big splashy cases."

"Brogan and Tinney gave you the straight dope? They weren't cute and holding back anything, such as a confession?"

"That Reed kid wasn't confessing to anything. He screamed his innocence as they led him away."

I signaled Louie to refill our glasses, and while he was doing so I asked Ben to give me the story of the murder. "Tinney's official version and any comments you care to throw in of your own."

Ben talked the way he wrote for the *Daily News*. "The rubout took place a week ago in Studio 6B at Radio City. The cast had just finished the dress rehearsal of the broadcast. That night the yarn from *Detective Fitzroy's Casebook* was a shoot-'em-up titled 'Murder at the World's Fair.' There was an hour or so before the program was to go on the air and everyone had left the studio except Worthington. He's not only the star of that little weekly melodrama but also the creator and the owner of the show. Worthington is quite a big shot in the radio business. Owns a couple of programs besides the detective show. He has one of those adventure programs for kids that you hear late in the afternoon when the kiddies are coming home from school and ought to be doing their homework instead of listening to radio serials. He also owns a soap opera. As a packager of shows, he makes a deal with sponsors and brings the shows to the networks. He's a perfectionist. *Was* a perfectionist. A gold-plated prick, from what I hear."

"Miss Skeffington hinted he never won any popularity contests."

"When was the boss ever popular, Harry?"

"So, the show had just finished rehearsing and—"

"Worthington remained in the studio alone on six going over the script. The door to the control room on seven was ajar and one of those guided tours that they run at Radio City was passing by. The kid leading the tour heard a shot. Naturally, he assumed it was a sound effect. It startled some of the tourists, so the kid—Robby Miller's his name—had to explain that it was just a sound effect and not a real gun. Only thing was, it was a real gun and a real bullet, as the cast found out when they returned to the studio just before it was time for the program to go on the air. There was Worthington sprawled on the floor with a bullet through his head. He was shot at six-oh-five P.M."

"How do you know the time that exactly?"

"Because Robby Miller heard the shot as he led the tour past the control room to Studio 6B at precisely six-oh-five. They run a lot of tours through Radio City and they do it on schedule. Miller's tour left the mezzanine at six sharp. It takes five minutes to reach the door to the control room on the seventh floor. The control room is a floor above the studio and looks down into it. Miller and the tourists heard the shot as they passed the door."

"A pistol shot?"

"The gun that killed Worthington was a revolver used for sound effects. It was on the floor beside his body. It contained five blanks and one empty shell. It was a thirty-eight-caliber Smith and Wesson police special."

"What about fingerprints?"

"The gun was wiped clean. Not even the prints of the sound-effects man. His name is Jerry Nolan and he's in the clear because he was working on another program at the time. Sound men do that, apparently. They work shows back to back."

"But he left his sound-effects equipment in the studio where Worthington was shot?"

"Each studio has its own sound-effects equipment."

"So anybody could have gotten the gun, put in a real round, and shot Worthington."

"The cops' theory is that David Reed—he's the announcer on the show and is Worthington's understudy—returned to the studio and blasted Worthington. There'd been bad blood between them. Noisy arguments."

"About what?"

"Probably who was to be Worthington's successor on the program."

"Successor?"

"Derek Worthington was about to ditch New York for a new career in Hollywood."

"He was giving up the detective show?"

"He'd signed a fat contract with Monogram Pictures to make a series of *Detective Fitzroy* movies. That meant he had to pick someone to take over the role on radio. Reed figured it was rightfully his because he'd been the understudy to Worthington, only Worthington let it be known that Reed was not going to land the part."

"So Reed kills Worthington? It's a motive but an awfully weak one."

"Guys have killed for a lot less than a juicy starring role on one of the hottest radio dramas on the air."

"What about the rest of the cast?"

"Oh, nobody liked Worthington and more than a few were pissed off that he wasn't taking any of them to Hollywood, but they all have concrete alibis for the time of the murder."

"Maybe somebody else . . . ?"

"Harry, the killer knew about the gun, knew that Worthington always hung around the studio between rehearsals and broadcast time, knew the ins and outs of Radio City, knew how to get into that studio and away from it after the murder without being seen. It has to have been somebody from the program, and the only one who can't verify his whereabouts at six-oh-five P.M. is David Reed."

"Where does he say he was?"

"He claims he went out for a stroll to get some fresh air and that he spent most of the hour watching the skaters on the rink in Rockefeller Plaza."

"Alone?"

"Well, he says he was surrounded by hundreds of people also watching the skaters and admiring the Christmas decorations, but they were all strangers. There's no one to identify him as being where he said he was. It's not as if he were a movie actor whose face Mr. John Q. Public would recognize. David Reed was famous as a name and a voice, not a face."

"How come he didn't spend that hour between the rehearsal and the broadcast with his girl friend?"

"Apparently they had a tiff." Ben shrugged and sipped his Knickerbocker beer. Setting it down as gently as if it were liquid gold, he said, "Miss Skeffington was having a bite to eat with Rita DeLong. She's the gal who plays the studio organ that provides the mood music for the show. They were in the cafeteria at the time of the murder."

"So, the layout was this: Worthington is in Studio 6B on the sixth floor. At six-oh-five P.M. a tour is going past the open door of the control room—"

"On the seventh floor. The control rooms are one floor up with a big window looking down on the studio. That gives the producer and technician a clear view of the whole studio."

"But if a shot is fired in a soundproof studio on the sixth floor, how can it be heard in the hallway on the seventh?"

"One of the microphones in the studio was turned on."

"That seems odd."

"Odd or not, one of the mikes was on. The control

room technician pointed that out to the police. He says it happened sometimes. An engineer thinks a mike is off but the switch is on and the pot—that's what they call the volume control knob—is turned up."

"And thanks to that open mike we know the precise time of the murder because a tour was going past the control room and heard it."

"That's what happened."

"Some coincidence."

"Well," said Ben as he lifted his beer, "you know what Hamlet said. 'Murder, though it have no tongue, will speak.' In this case, it spoke through that open mike."

Early the next morning I located Detective Bill Tinney amid the long rows of brown file cabinets in the fingerprints section of the police department's Criminal Identification Bureau upstairs in the Police Academy Building at Broome and Centre streets, a clean-cut structure standing out in bold contrast to the clutter of fire escapes, washlines, and crowded stoops of the tired old tenements sprawled across Manhattan's Lower East Side. I knew the neighborhood well, a noisy and teeming stretch of dreary poverty around the gray-faced and somber five-story pile of stone that was police headquarters at 240 Centre Street, flanked on the north and south by Broome and Grand streets and on the west by Center Market Place, where Ben Turner and the other denizens of the world of crime reporting hung out in the Press Shack and scrambled for the latest sensation to be found on what they called the police blotter, the official record of the misdeeds of the citizens of O. Henry's "Bagdad-on-the-Subway."

Not everything that the police know about a case goes in the record and on the blotter, and while Bill Tinney was one of those cops who never lied outright to the press, he was still a cop who would be more willing to provide the off-the-record stuff about a case to a former cop and friend than to a reporter, so before I went any further along in the interests of Maggie Skeffington, I had to talk to Tinney. My familiar face and old friendships got me in where reporters couldn't go. Bill greeted me with a big smile and an iron handshake and a look in his eye that told me he knew I was working on a case, but he was flabbergasted when I told him what that case was. "What the hell is there in the Reed case for you, Harry? It's cut and dried." The smile on his Irish face widened to a grin. "It's that Skeffington dame. Right?"

"You get the Sherlock Holmes Award for pure deduction, Bill."

He closed the file drawer he'd been rummaging in and leaned against the cabinet. "I figured she was the type to follow her emotions, but I'm surprised as hell to find Harry MacNeil marching into the fray on her behalf. I thought she'd latch on to one of those shady characters who give the private detective business a bad name. Believe me, Harry, David Reed's guilty. It's only a matter of time until he breaks down and admits it."

"What you've got is pretty flimsy, Bill."

"I've had flimsier cases and gotten convictions. Reed will crack sooner or later."

"The old third degree?" I was kidding.

"Harry, Harry, you know we got rid of the rubber hoses long ago."

"Your case rests on Reed's inability to prove that he

-18-

was watching the ice skaters at Rockefeller Plaza at the time of the murder."

"Plus a pretty strong motive."

"To kill someone just because he won't hire you for a job? Come on, Bill."

"He did threaten to kill Worthington."

"Threatening Derek Worthington appears to have been as popular a pastime as Monopoly. There's not a damned thing in Reed's background to show that he had the guts to carry out that threat. David Reed is a Mr. Milquetoast, from what I hear."

Tinney came up straight. "You heard wrong, Harry. Young Mr. Reed possesses a hair-trigger temper and a record to prove it."

"A police record?"

"Two cases of assault in the last year alone. He bashed a waiter at Lindy's one night last August. Johnny Broderick happened to be there at the time and cold-cocked him when Reed started throwing punches in Johnny's direction. The only thing that kept Reed out of the pokey that time was the fact that neither the waiter nor Broderick would press charges. Okay, maybe that was just barroom-brawl stuff, but in November he assaulted none other than Derek Worthington in the Rainbow Room. The network people put the kibosh on that one. Mr. Milquetoast? Not by a long shot, Harry. The boyfriend of your pretty client brought a thirty-eight caliber bullet into that studio, slipped it into the sound-effects pistol, and fired that bullet into Worthington's head. That's murder one, Harry. Premeditated murder. And David Reed's going to the chair for it."

"Any moderately sharp defense lawyer could make a shambles out of that case, Bill."

"Then I'd suggest that you advise your client to hire one. I'm not one to take the bread off your table, Harry, but if you continue working this case you'll just be stealing that Skeffington gal's dough. On the subject of lawyers, Reed's gonna need more than a moderately sharp attorney 'cause the district attorney's office has assigned this one to Timothy Brogan. It's just his kind of case. Lots of headlines and an easy conviction. Another scalp on the belt of a guy who's got his eyes on a political future. Take the advice of an old pal, Harry. Get off this *Titanic* before she sails. Do Reed a favor and tell him the jig's up and that his only hope is to come clean and throw himself on the mercy of the court. The smartest thing that guy can do right now is give us a confession."

I appreciated how Tinney felt. For a cop there was nothing as tidy as a confession. Persuading a suspect to admit guilt could save a cop a lot of legwork. There were still plenty of cops on the police force who would go beyond persuasive words to get a confession. Despite Commissioner Lew Valentine's efforts to clean up the department, there were those cops who turned to muscle to get a confession. Fortunately for David Reed, Bill Tinney was never a cop who resorted to fists or the rubber hose to close a case.

The suspect in the murder of Derek Worthington was locked up in the Tombs and that's where I headed. There'd been a city prison at Centre and Franklin streets for a hundred years. The original lockup was officially called the Halls of Justice, but it got the name the Tombs because the design of the building had been copied from a picture of an ancient Egyptian mausoleum in a book by an author from Hoboken who'd been on a tour of the land of the pharaohs. The twentieth-century building erected by the city of New York to lock up its miscreants was referred to as a house of detention officially, but to cops and those they booked into the jail it was and always would be the Tombs.

It's not a long walk from Centre and Broome streets to the Tombs, but the stroll from a cell on death row at Sing Sing to the little green room where they keep the electric chair is a lot shorter. It was that brief passage from life to death that played on my mind after I left Bill Tinney poking through his fingerprint files. I'd had plenty of opportunities as a cop to attend executions at Sing Sing but I declined all of them. A lot of my fellow members of the police department happily accepted the invitations, especially the ones that were finales to cases they'd worked on. I understood how they felt. A lot of those cops had seen their brother officers killed in the line of duty. All had been witnesses to the atrocities that human beings inflict on one another, but I never had any desire to watch anyone strapped into a chair while bolts of man-made lightning shot through him. Walking down Centre Street to interview David Reed at the Tombs, I could not dismiss the likelihood that Reed would wind up in that chair at Sing Sing. For whatever reason, the forces of law and order in the greatest city in the world had decided that Reed was guilty of the murder of Derek Worthington. Walking toward the Tombs to see for myself the object of this impressive marshaling of the forces of justice, I couldn't avoid comparing that array of power to the pitiful plight of one man in the Tombs who had nothing going for him but his insistence that he was innocent and the blind faith of the young woman who had come to me. "The help of the hopeless."

My estimation of David Reed's prospects were as gloomy as the December overcast when I turned onto Franklin from Centre and went through the entrance of the grim facade of the city's prison, but by the time I found myself sitting in a Spartanly furnished room where prisoners came to meet their lawyers, and waiting for David Reed to be brought from his cell, I found myself thinking about Bill Tinney's last words to me. "The best thing that guy can do right now is make a confession."

Best thing for whom? For Reed? Confess on the chance that a judge might show a little mercy and reduce his sentence from the chair to life in prison? Or for Tinney and D.A. Brogan and that awesome panoply of prosecutorial power whose case was so shaky that they feared they would not get a conviction without a confession? All along I'd been told that the case against Reed was open and shut, cut and dried. But was it? Maybe not. Nothing was open and shut as long as there existed in the law of the greatest city in the world that wonderful admonition that every judge deliver to every jury of twelve men good and true, that they have to be convinced beyond the shadow of a doubt of the guilt of the accused.

That was what I would be looking for when I talked to David Reed. The shadow of a doubt.

## 4

"I'm at a loss to know why you're here, Mr. MacNeil."

Even without the background effects of bursts of gunfire, the squeal of tires, the wail of police sirens, and the swell of sinister music played on the studio organ that opened *Detective Fitzroy's Casebook* every week, there was no mistaking the voice that proclaimed to millions of radio listeners, "Once again the forces of law, order, and justice swing into action. . . ."

"I've been hired by Maggie Skeffington."

"Dear sweet Maggie."

"She tells me you're not the type to commit murder."

"I didn't do it, Mr. MacNeil."

"How old are you, Mr. Reed?"

"Twenty-three. Why?"

"You seem a little on the young side to be a network radio announcer." If I'd been asked to guess his age I would have put it a couple of years younger. Maybe it was his thatch of straw-blond hair or the big doe eyes or the turned-up nose, his central-casting Andy Hardy earnestness, but the kid came across as a boy so square-cut and squeaky-clean that I had no problem understanding why Maggie Skeffington would describe him as the kindest, most considerate, gentlest man she ever knew.

"I've been a radio announcer since I was eighteen, Mr. MacNeil," he was saying as I looked him over. The blue eyes were direct, but there was a hint of hurt in them and I realized that I had bruised his professional ego by suggesting that mere age had anything to do with talent in radio announcing. "I've worked at radio stations in Cleveland, Pittsburgh, and Philadelphia and I've been on the air in New York for almost three years. I've been the announcer on *Fitzroy's Casebook* for over a year."

"No offense," I said with a shrug. "You just sound older than you look." I cracked a peacemaking smile. "People you hear on the radio never look the way they sound. I assumed you were older, is all." I took out a pack of Luckies and gave him one. He grabbed it as if he had been waiting all his life for someone to give him a cigarette. I slid the pack across the table to him. "Keep 'em."

"I could use the matches, too," he said, flashing a little apologetic smile. He stuffed the green pack and the matches in the breast pocket of his gray Tombs uniform. "Thanks." For an instant the voice that sounded so manly and authoritative on the radio quavered, and it was easy to see that David Reed was a scared kid. "How is Maggie?" he asked bravely through a puff of Luckies smoke.

"Maggie is okay."

He took away the Lucky and smiled again, but this time it was a joyful smile, the expression of a guy who couldn't quite believe he'd had the luck to be loved by Maggie Skeffington. "She actually hired you?"

-23-

"I told her that if you should turn out to be the innocent victim you claim you are, I'd send *you* the bill."

The cigarette dropped to the floor and he ground it out. "I didn't do it! That's the truth. I wasn't anywhere near Studio 6B when they say it happened. I was watching the skaters on the rink."

"Unfortunately no one can back you up on that."

"It's a city of strangers, Mr. MacNeil." The line sounded like something from one of Derek Worthington's poorer scripts, but as cliché as it was it served to underscore for me how demoralized Reed was. There was in the way he said it—as if the words had been dipped in vinegar—a forlorn sadness that set off in my head a little chirp of credulity.

"If you didn't kill Worthington, who do you suppose might have?"

"I have no idea. I can't believe that anyone would actually murder him."

"You threatened to."

He suddenly laughed and I supposed it was from surprise that I knew so much about him. "That was just something I said. I never meant it. You know how people say things they don't mean."

"Sure I do, but in your case, the man you threatened to kill has wound up dead and you don't have an alibi. What was there that made you so angry that you threatened to kill him?"

"We just had heated words over his decision to give the Fitzroy part to someone else."

"In the right prosecutor's hands that could add up to a convincing case for murder."

"I didn't kill him. I told you."

"Telling me won't save you from the chair."

He dug out the pack of Luckies and lit up again. "Derek was a man who got other people mad at him. I was no different."

"Maybe you were angry enough to kill him."

"No part on the radio is worth a man's life, Mr. Mac-
Neil. Sure, I wanted to play the Fitzroy role. I was good
at it when I stood in for Derek at times when he couldn't
be there at rehearsals."

"Did you ever play the part on the air?"

"Derek never missed a show."

"If you were so good why'd he turn you down as his
replacement when he went to Hollywood?"

"Derek did things like that. Just to hurt people."

"Why didn't he just fire you?"

"Because I was part of the cast."

"What's that mean?"

"Derek believed he had put together the best cast in
radio. He saw us as his family, and in a way we were.
We're a repertory company."

"And you were all so good that he'd never break up
the company?"

"Yes."

"He'd punish you and treat you like shit, but he'd
never fire you and you wouldn't quit? C'mon."

"You have to understand how special that program
is, Mr. MacNeil."

"Somebody in that repertory company, that little
closely knit family, shot the head of the family to death.
Some family."

"I refuse to believe anyone in the cast killed Derek."

"You can believe what you like, but the cops and the
D.A. believe you're the culprit. What the hell were you
doing out at the skating rink that night? How come you
weren't with Maggie?"

"We had a row."

"About what?"

"I can't even remember it was so trivial. It was just a
boy-girl fight, you know?"

"Yeah, I know."

"So while Maggie and the others went to the cafeteria as usual between the rehearsal and the show, I went out for some fresh air."

"It's the little mistakes that we pay for. Remember that before you have another boy-girl fight and then go for a walk."

"If I'd known that someone was going to pick that moment to murder Derek, I assure you I would not have wandered off alone."

"Sorry. I didn't mean to be sarcastic."

"Hell, you're right. My temper got me into this."

"Are you certain no one can vouch for you being at the rink?"

"Nobody. I was just another face in the crowd, believe me."

"I believe you."

"God, what a mess."

For an instant the Andy Hardy in him veered close to tears, but the twenty-three-year-old veteran of the radio business whose voice was almost as well known to the American radio audience as Franklin D. Roosevelt's regained control of itself, and the network radio announcer's voice spoke out clear and strong. "I appreciate the fix I'm in, Mr. MacNeil, but I promise you I'm innocent."

"When the rehearsal was over you had a spat with Maggie and took off for the great outdoors of Rockefeller Plaza."

"I wanted to be alone. I had some thinking to do."

"About what?"

"Just . . . things."

"So you put on your overcoat and went out to the plaza and—"

"No."

"No?"

"I didn't put on my coat. I didn't start out for the skating rink. I went down to the lobby and was walking around there and on an impulse I went outside."

"Yet no one saw you, not even in the elevator—"

"I walked down to the lobby."

"Great! Why?"

"I walked down. I did that sometimes rather than wait for an elevator."

"And you walked through the lobby of the RCA Building and out to the plaza and no one in the world saw you who could verify all this?"

"That's right."

"On the other hand, maybe you didn't walk down to the lobby and out to the rink. On the other hand, maybe you returned to Studio 6B as you had planned to all along and shot Derek Worthington to death."

"I didn't want him dead."

"You said you did. You said so in public."

"That was just words."

"Those words could land you in the electric chair." He looked defeated. "Have you got a lawyer?"

"A public defender."

"The D.A. will make mincemeat out of him."

"But I didn't kill anyone. I wouldn't've done anything to hurt Maggie. Please believe me."

Which is exactly what my predicament came down to: whether to believe Bill Tinney with his painstakingly collected police evidence and his lifetime of solving crimes or take the word of a couple of kids whose entire lives amounted to nothing more substantial than ether.

# 5

When I got uptown again after my rather depressing chat with David Reed, the afternoon papers were black with big headlines about the final act in a drama that had been holding the world's attention for almost a week. The British navy had managed to bottle up the giant Nazi battleship *Graf Spee* in the harbor of Montevideo, Uruguay, after a thunderous battle that had left the British ships *Exeter*, *Achilles*, and *Ajax* damaged but still seaworthy enough to be a threat to the German ship if she came out to sea again. There was never any doubt whose side the New York newspapers were on. In a town where the mayor regularly denounced the Nazis as two-bit gangsters and chiselers and where Winchell referred in his columns to the rulers of Germany as Ratzis and where there was a large population of Jews, there had developed a pro-British cheering section during the standoff off the River Plate. Now the newspaper headlines crowed with glee that the *Graf Spee* had been scuttled rather than suffer the ignominy of being blown out of the water by the Royal Navy. Chalk up one loss for Hitler, the world's number-one gangster, I said to myself. I bought a paper from a kid hawking them as I came out of the subway.

There was another item about another gangster in the paper that interested me that afternoon. Down in federal court they were winding up the government's case against Louis Buchalter, known as Lepke. His lawyer, William W. Kleinman, had actually told the jury in his summation that they ought to overlook what he called "the myth" of Lepke. Some myth! Lepke had come up from a sneak thief as a kid to be the kingpin of a fifty-million-dollar-a-year rackets business that included narcotics smuggling, the rap he was standing trial for. I'd known this bum since he came to the attention of Jacob

("Little Augie") Orgen and after that when Lepke was only one of Little Augie's protégés. Also tutored in crime by Little Augie were such underworld luminaries as Lucky Luciano, Waxey Gordon, and Legs Diamond. In the summer, when the heat got too great from the feds, the New York police, and the mob itself, Lepke had arranged to give himself up to none other than J. Edgar Hoover, the head of the FBI, with Winchell acting as go-between. Now the cockroach Lepke was sitting in court and listening to his mouthpiece beg a jury not to consider Lepke's bloody history because it was nothing more than a myth! I could easily imagine Police Commissioner Lew Valentine in his office on Centre Street screaming his head off over this latest incident in which a gangster was being portrayed as a misunderstood popular hero. All through the years of Prohibition, when the gangsters came into their own and when the newspapers played them up as dashing and colorful characters, Valentine had fought against the guys La Guardia called tinhorns and chiselers, and Valentine had suffered for it, being stuck in posts where he couldn't do any harm to the mobsters who had friends in high places, including City Hall and Centre Street headquarters. Now that Valentine was La Guardia's commissioner much of that bunkum about gangsters being glamorous was being put to rest. Muss 'em up, was Valentine's rule. He was also working hard to get the rotten apples out of the police department, and I was glad to see that honest cops like Bill Tinney were finally getting a chance to show that the New York Police Department was entitled to the nickname "the finest."

Tinney was one of the best cops on the force, a fact that didn't bode well for the scared kid I'd just left down in the Tombs. Tinney's meticulous police work, combined with the sharp courtroom tactics of D.A. Tim Brogan, would probably land David Reed in the death house even if Tinney didn't get the confession that he'd wanted me to persuade the kid to provide. I'd been prepared to go either way in my chat with Reed, but I'd heard that little chirp of credulity that had always been a reliable guide to me in all my years as a detective, both official and private. Instinct, I called it. For Maggie Skeffington it was woman's intuition. Whatever you called it, it wasn't evidence and evidence is what matters in a courtroom.

## 6

When I called Maggie to tell her that I'd paid a visit to her boyfriend in the Tombs, she insisted on coming up to my office to hear the details. It took her less than ten minutes to walk over from the Hotel Bristol. She looked like a model in an ad for the latest fashions for the smart junior miss about town, the look that "pert" seemed to describe best, with a wisp of a hat that seemed to be nothing but a scrap of white veil, a navy-blue skirt and jacket, and a ruffled white blouse buttoned to the neck. "You caught me just as I came in," she said breathlessly. "I'd been to an audition for a new detective program that Phillips H. Lord is going to be doing on Mutual." She sat with her legs crossed and her black purse in her lap. "With the future of *Fitzroy's Casebook* in doubt I thought I'd better take a look at the options." She took a deep breath. "How is David? How did he look? The last time I saw him he was so pale."

"He looked fine." I lied. There was no point in telling her the kid looked damned scared and that there was every reason for him to be. "He seems to be holding up well. First thing he asked was how you are."

"Typical of him to be worried about me instead of himself."

"David's much younger than I expected."

"Radio's a young person's business. Every actor on the show is in his or her twenties. Even Derek wasn't that old—thirty-three, I believe—but to the rest of us he was the wise old veteran, a kind of hero figure because Derek was a pioneer in radio. I don't know what will happen to *Fitzroy's Casebook* now."

"It was going to go on without him, what with him going to Hollywood."

"Yes, because Derek woud have remained in control even from the coast."

"Why didn't he just take the radio show to the coast with him?"

"Derek wanted it kept here because New York has the best radio actors. At least that's what he said. We were grateful to him for that. I doubt if many of us—if any—would have gone out to Los Angeles had he decided to move the show. Also, I think, the sponsor wanted the show kept here. J. William Richards, owner of the Mellow-Gold Coffee Company, is a radio buff. He comes into Radio City frequently to watch when the show is on the air. I think he wanted to keep the show here so he could come in and sit in the control room and watch us at work. Poor J. William was terribly distraught over Derek's death. He respected Derek and was Derek's number-one backer."

"Well, it's nice to know Worthington had one person who didn't hate his guts."

"I don't think anyone actually hated Derek—"

"One person hated him enough to blow his brains out."

"I see your point, but the rest of us just had our troubles with Derek. David was going through a difficult time with Derek, but David didn't hate him. Radio's a business full of temperamental people. There's always a clash of egos, but everyone in the cast was devoted to the show and wouldn't let personal problems with Derek get in the way. We understood that Derek would not permit anyone to work on the show who was not a complete professional at all times. The slightest trace of nonprofessionalism was enough for Derek to ban an actor or a technician from all his shows."

"Did you ever see that happen?"

"Only once. One of the bit players came back drunk from dinner just before showtime. Derek fired him on the spot."

"What happened with the part the guy was playing?"

"Derek portrayed it himself. It was an amazing demonstration of Derek's genius. As deplorable as Derek could be as a human being, he was a master at radio. In a few minutes he rewrote the bit part so it would play as a Frenchman. Then he carried it off with unbelievable skill. There was a whole page of dialogue in which Derek as Fitzroy and Derek as the Frenchman carried on a conversation. Of course, the actor who was drunk was banned from all of Derek's shows. Derek had the fellow blackballed in the business."

"Worthington had that much clout?"

"He did. An actor's pathetic alcoholism cut no ice with Derek. He'd been unprofessional and that was that. I suppose he regarded it as disloyalty. Derek could never forgive unprofessionalism, disloyalty, or ingratitude."

"Do you have any ideas what that actor he fired is doing now?"

Maggie made a face. "He's a talent agent. If you think private eyes are sleazy, Mr. MacNeil, you should meet a few talent agents."

"I'd like to meet this one. And the name's Harry. Where's this fellow have his office? What's his name?"

"He's Freddy Shoemaker and he's got an office on Forty-second Street. Why on earth talk to him?"

"Well, it seems to me that a guy who's been fired, humiliated, and blackballed in the broadcasting business and who knows his way around Derek Worthington's radio shows had the motive and the means to bump Worthington off. I'd like to find out if he also had the opportunity."

Maggie beamed and threw her arms around me. "Oh, Harry, how wonderful of you!"

"Then," said I, basking in the circle of Maggie's arms around my neck, "I'll want to meet the rest of the cast of *Detective Fitzroy's Casebook*."

"That'll be easy. We rehearse tomorrow at Radio City. I'll bring you along." Uncoiling her arms and sitting again in the oak chair by my desk, she looked at me with a light in her eyes that told me she was convinced that I was on the verge of proving that her boyfriend was innocent of murder. I didn't have the heart to tell her that talking to all of these people was groping in the dark.

"Now that you've talked to David, you do believe he's innocent?"

"I'm giving him the benefit of the doubt. That's as far as I can go, Maggie."

That pretty face with the Miss Molloy voice was crestfallen. "I'm going to stand by him, Harry, no matter what."

"You mustn't get his hopes up. You mustn't get your hopes up."

She shot to her feet again with the starry-eyed faith of a little girl who knows her father's broke and can't possibly afford the big expensive fancy doll she wants for Christmas but, like a kid in a Damon Runyon yarn, will never not believe in miracles during the season of the birth of the Babe of Bethlehem. "David is innocent, Harry," she exclaimed, "and he and I know you'll prove it. You will prove it, Harry?"

"If he's innocent, he's got nothing to worry about."

"Oh, he is, Harry. He is!" She gave me a hug and kiss and dashed out, leaving me in my drafty office on the fourth floor at the rear of the brownstone that housed the Onyx Club. The first office I'd opened when I turned in my old NYPD badge for a private investigator's license had been above the original Onyx across the street and a few doors west, until the building burned down one blustery night in February 1935. After that I'd hung up my license and my hat in half a dozen rooms on the West Side until I discovered another vacancy over the Onyx at 62 West Fifty-second.

The block of hot jazz clubs looked cold and bleak in the daylight as I headed toward Times Square to locate Freddy Shoemaker. The shoulder-to-shoulder joints of The Street resembled nothing like the glamour spots they were made out to be in the gossip columns. The biggest names in Jazz were painted on billboards outside the clubs, but there wasn't a jazzman in sight on that cold-sun afternoon in December.

At Radio City Music Hall the line waiting to get in for the Christmas extravaganza at the Showplace of the Nation was four abreast and curved around onto Fiftieth Street all the way to the corner opposite the glittering Rockefeller Center tree, where David Reed insisted he had spent the moment when someone was putting a bullet through Derek Worthington's brain.

# 7

I looked up Freddy Shoemaker in the book and then found the office of the actor-turned-agent five floors up at the top of a grim and narrow building sandwiched between the blazing lights of the marquees that were elbow to elbow in the block between Times Square and Eighth Avenue, the gaudiest conglomeration of movie houses in the world, which drew tourists by the millions, so many visitors that it was boasted that if you stood on the corner at Broadway and Forty-second, sooner or later you would meet everybody you knew in the world. While you were waiting you could keep up on the news by reading the headlines that crawled around the triangular Times Building, the ribbon of lights spelling out that day the saga of the Royal Navy's victory over the *Graf Spee* along the coast of South America, the war going on between brave little Finland and the Russians, and the efforts by a group called the National Women's Party, which was trying to persuade Congress to pass an equal rights amendment on behalf of women. The building where Freddy Shoemaker hung his hat was loaded with agents' offices, and I was reminded as I climbed the stairs of an actor friend of mine who complained that an agent was someone you never heard from again. The friend was waiting on tables at Lindy's at the time and dishing out wisecracks to the customers. He claimed to be the Lindy's waiter who came up with the answer to the guy who asked what a fly was doing in his soup. "Why, I believe it's the backstroke, sir."

I knocked on Shoemaker's door.

"It's open."

Standing in the doorway and looking across a square office that was even smaller and shabbier than mine, the man behind the desk was, I decided, shifty, oily, devious, suspicious, cutthroat, and moneygrubbing—all the attributes I'd want to find in an agent if I needed one. Small, wiry, and skinny as a pipe cleaner, Shoemaker had on a gray plaid suit, white shirt, and a yellow bow tie. Beneath a bird's beak nose he sported a toothbrush-bristle moustache. Gray light struggled through a grimy window and painted a silver halo at the edges of his thinning gray hair. His desk was elbow-deep in stacks of papers, file folders, and eight-by-ten glossies of aspiring talents. Amid the pile rose an upright telephone like a leafless tree in a snowy meadow. The walls of the office were festooned with advertising cards for Broadway shows and movies, front pages of *Variety*, and framed photos of young actors with the same earnest and clean-cut jaws and direct honest eyes of David Reed, the hopeful faces of young men whose dreams were filled with starring roles on Broadway, the radio, and the silver screen. Most of the photos were signed with expressions of gratitude for the help Freddy Shoemaker had given in launching or extending their careers. For no reason other than the fact that I had taken an immediate gut-felt dislike for Shoemaker, I assumed that Shoemaker had written the sentiments and signed the photos himself.

He looked at me the way most people looked at bill collectors. "What's your beef?" he growled.

"If I had a beef," I growled back as I crossed his office, "I wouldn't't've knocked."

Shoemaker grunted a laugh and reached for a Chesterfield. He took his time lighting it and then blew the smoke my way. "Are you one of Johnny Broderick's flatfeet? I don't talk to flatfeet without a warrant." He rocked back in his chair with the cigarette dangling wise-guy fashion from the corner of his slit of a mouth. I flipped one of my business cards on his desk. He picked it up, read it, and tore it in half. "Get lost, shamus."

"Where were you Sunday night a week ago at six o'clock?"

"At Saint Malachy's making a novena for asshole private dicks."

"We can have a polite conversation or we can have the other kind, Shoemaker."

He ground out the Chesterfield, bent, opened a desk drawer, and lifted out a half-empty bottle of Old Crow. Pouring the liquor into a water glass that hadn't seen dishwater in a year, he did not offer to share the whiskey. He drank half the glass before he asked, "What are we talking about here? What's so important about last Sunday night?" Then dawn broke in his head. He smiled. "Ah, that's when somebody blew Derek Worthington's brains out all over the floor of a radio studio. When I heard, I went out and celebrated that night along with half the radio actors in New York." The sun rose higher in his cloudy brain. "Say, do you think that I—?" He exploded into laughter. "That's funny!"

"I still haven't heard where you were six o'clock that Sunday night."

"I was working."

"Where? Doing what?"

Shoemaker emptied the filthy water glass and poured more Old Crow. "What I was doing don't matter. I've got witnesses if it comes to that."

"I thought this was going to be a polite conversation," I whispered, leaning across his desk.

"Fuck off."

I slapped the glass out of his hand. It flew across the room and shattered against a filing cabinet and cut little rivulets of whiskey down the grimy wall. "Don't make me get physical, Freddy."

Trembling, he reached for the Old Crow bottle and clutched it to his chest, hugging it like a Teddy bear. "I was in the Dynamic Film Studios on West Forty-eighth Street from noon till after midnight. You can check it out. I've gotten into film directing lately. I'm quite good at it."

I straightened up and smiled. "Films, huh? What kind of films? The ones where the girls wear masks and the guys have moustaches and keep their socks on?"

"Legit, MacNeil. Legit films. You can check it out."

"I will."

Relaxing, Shoemaker set the bottle on the desk, but he kept a hand around it. For a moment I felt really sorry for him. The glass I'd smashed was probably his only one. "Name some of the people who could have wanted Worthington dead."

"The list, Mr. MacNeil, would consist of more than

half the entire membership of the American Federation of Radio Artists. You want suspects, ask the union for a list. The whole town hated that son of a bitch."

"He blackballed *you*."

Shoemaker cracked a smile and drew the bottle toward him again. "Things have worked out okay for me. I'm in films now. So, you see, maybe I owe something to Worthington after all." He lifted the bottle to his lips and took a gurgling swig. A little trickle of Old Crow made its way down to his chin. He put down the bottle tenderly and wagged a bony finger at me. "That kid they've arrested for the murder? David Reed? Well, take my word for it, that kid didn't do it. I know that. You know it, else why are you here harassing me? You want to find the real killer, is that it? Well, start with the people closest to that bastard Worthington. Never knew a guy who could make enemies as easily as that shmuck."

"Name me a few names."

"The producer, Miles Flannagan, had reason. He would have been left high and dry once Worthington went to the coast. Worthington was going to fire his ass and get a new producer for that crime show. And nobody—nobody—is going to hire Flannagan, believe me."

"Who else?"

"That cunt who writes some of the shows. Veronica Blake. Worthington was going to drop her, too. Did you know that Worthington was banging that broad? Well, he was, and that gave somebody else a motive. I refer to Worthington's co-star, the one and only Jason Patrick, who, I'm sure you know, plays the role of Sergeant O'Donnell. Dear sweet Veronica is Patrick's current heartthrob, don't you know? Oh, there are plenty of suspects, MacNeil, so why the fuck are you coming around bothering me?" He almost sobbed the last words.

Truth when you hear it rings like crystal and it was ringing loudly in that dingy office. Freddy Shoemaker hadn't killed Derek Worthington because he didn't have the guts to. "Is that all you have to tell me, Shoemaker?"

"You're a cop. Dig around. You'll come up with plenty of dirt on that guy. He was a regular tomcat. He was involved with that other cunt on the show."

"Rita DeLong, the organist?"

"Her, too, but that was a couple of years ago. Nah, I mean the new dame in the role of Miss Molloy. Maggie what's-her-name." He lifted his bottle again and took a swig. "Ask her how she happened to get that job and keep it."

"I don't believe you."

He laughed. "Are you sweet on her or something?"

I was on him hard, slamming him out of the chair and onto his ass on the floor, my hands making a knot out of his loud lapels. "Explain yourself, cockroach."

Even though he was terrified he managed a cackling laugh. "Hey, MacNeil, is she something to you? Huh?"

"Tell me what you meant by that crack about her getting and keeping her job."

"Surely you've heard of the casting couch, Mac-Neil?"

My impulse was to smash his face. Instead, I smashed his bottle of Old Crow.

# 8

The Crossroads of the World looked just as advertised when I stepped out into the carnival-midway glitter and glare of Forty-second Street. Night settled early in New York in mid-December, but Forty-second was brighter than daylight as I swung west toward Eighth Avenue. Jack Dempsey's joint across from Madison Square Garden was my destination for two reasons. First, I was hungry. Second, I wanted to have a chat with Johnny Broderick about David Reed's fisticuffs in Lindy's in August. Just as anybody could either find me or learn my whereabouts by dropping in at the Onyx, you could always go to Dempsey's if you were looking for Johnny Broderick.

During the years of Damon Runyon's gold rush, plenty of criminals had been made into stars by the newspaper boys, but there was really only one cop who got the celebrity treatment and that was Broderick. In fact, his name became synonymous with physical law enforcement. To "Broderick" a bad guy was to manhandle him, to put it mildly. Broderick was not a cop who needed Lew Valentine to tell him to muss up the tinhorns and chiselers. Broderick had been doing that for years. A cross between a middleweight and a lightweight, Broderick was always ready to rush in with fists where cops with guns were hesitant. Johnny Broderick didn't need to hear the words of Commissioner Mulrooney, who once told his cops, "I do not want you to have any hesitancy if you come upon a man who is a criminal or a racketeer and you have reason to believe he is armed. I want you to pull first and give it to him if he makes any attempt to get you. Do not be the last to draw."

Drawing a gun was not what Johnny Broderick became famous for, however. The brawny detective was much more likely to wade into the crooks with fists flailing, a characteristic that grabbed a lot of headlines. This was at a time when it was open season on cops—sixty-one killed on duty between 1924 and 1930—but the underworld knew that the Broderick fists were his big weapons. They feared the Broderick fists more than any other cop's gun. All shoulders, burly arms, square jaw, nothing delighted him more than to crash through a door and charge a gang of crooks. For years on end, the cry "Broderick is coming" emptied any thieves' poolroom or low booze den.

While Broderick would relish his reputation as a two-fisted lawman and do nothing to knock down many spurious stories floated about him by admiring newspapermen, and while it was true that he had little use for the pistol and preferred to wade into crooks with arms flaying like a windmill, head down like a charging bull, he resorted to his gun when a gun made considerably more sense than knuckles.

On the afternoon of November 3, 1926, Broderick rushed to the Tombs with an army of cops, all loaded to the armpits, literally, with weapons. Broderick arrived with gun drawn and a bandolier of ammo slung over his broad shoulders to lend his presence to the force summoned to deal with an escape attempt at the city prison. A week earlier, guns and ammunition had been smuggled into the cells for the benefit of three of the worst desperadoes of the day—Hymie Amberg, Red McKenna, and Bobbie Berg, all veteran criminals and vicious gunmen who had reputations as tough guys. All three were staring long prison terms in the face. Making their break for freedom, they overpowered the guards, murdered a keeper, and then killed the warden. Inching toward the main gate of the Tombs, they met a rain of gunfire from the cops ringing the massive bastion. The trio fell back to a coal yard and fashioned a sooty fort to fend off the cops. Thousands of rounds were fired. The legendary neighborhood of the old Five Pointers gang again rang with the report of weapons. It was a war and a standoff. That is, until Broderick showed up on the scene and took charge of the problem.

No one in the NYPD could remember ever seeing anything like it. Broderick entered the coal yard alone. Crawling, he edged toward the fortress, firing his pistol as he advanced. He emptied the revolver once, reloaded, then sprang to his feet and charged like a hero in an incredibly melodramatic Hollywood script. By the time the raging detective scaled the coal pile, one of the escapers had put his gun to his own head and blown his brains out. The other two threw their weapons onto the coal and gave up.

The hero of these escapades was destroying a steak and baked potato when I sauntered into Jack Dempsey's place to ask about David Reed's kayo of a waiter at Lindy's last August. "Oh, that," chuckled Broderick between chews of his practically raw sirloin. "I've known lots of guys who wanted to deck one of Lindy's smarty-pants waiters, but the Reed kid's the only one I ever heard of doing it. It was nothing. The waiter was a pansy actor and apparently thought Reed was of a similar disposition. A lot of china got smashed and proprietor Mr. Leo Lindeman was upset and wanted to press charges, but I calmed him down. A flash in the pan. Nothing for a hotshot private dick to get excited about, Harry." He paused with a bloody slab of steak halfway between plate and mouth. "Or is it?"

"Reed's in the Tombs on a murder rap."

Broderick popped the steak in his mouth, chewed a moment, and swallowed hard. "The murder at Radio City."

"That's it. I don't believe the kid did it."

"Bill Tinney will wager next year's salary that he did."

"Bill's a good cop but he's wrong on this one."

"And Harry MacNeil's going to prove it?"

"Harry MacNeil's going to try."

"Must be a dame in the case."

"The dame is a very nice gal."

"Well, for what it's worth, Harry, I wouldn't have any problem believing the Reed kid could commit murder. It was sure in his eyes that night in Lindy's, and over something that most guys would have ignored. Not that the pansy waiter didn't have it coming to him, but this is New York and if every good-looking kid in town who had a pass made at him by a queer resorted to assault, there'd be no room in the lockups for the truly bad guys. Maybe the victim made a similar pass."

"Derek Worthington wasn't shot in a fit of anger. He was killed by someone who went to a lot of trouble to plan it and carry it out."

"Premeditation. Murder one. Reed'll fry for it if he did it." He chewed more steak and washed it down with beer from a huge stein. He wiped his lips and grinned. "Of course, if the kid can be gotten off, you're the one who'll do it, Harry. That's the sort of thing a man shouldn't undertake on an empty stomach. Be my guest."

With that he signaled for a waiter and ordered two steaks, one for me and another for himself. While we waited I asked him what he knew about Freddy Shoemaker.

"A real scumbag. To get the whole story on him you'll have to talk to the boys of the Vice Squad. He's gotten mixed up in some pretty sleazy businesses. The skin game, if you know what I mean. Stag films and the like. The Vice Squad's got its eye on him. What's he to you?"

"Derek Worthington fired him for being drunk."

"I'm not surprised, but if you're thinking of tagging Shoemaker with a murder rap, forget it. The bum hasn't got the guts."

"He's set himself up as a talent agent."

"Yeah, I know. That's where he recruits the girls and boys for his filthy movies. Don't worry about Shoemaker, we'll nail him. It won't be for murder one, but it'll be enough to send him up the river."

An hour later Broderick was off on a tour of his Broadway turf and I was heading for Swing Street. When

I walked into the Onyx the band was in fine fettle. Along about three in the morning the clarinetist gave me a wink and held out his instrument, an invitation I could never turn down. The music lasted until after four and I did pretty well in my turns, the murder of Derek Worthington the farthest thing from my mind, that is until I stepped down from the bandstand and returned to my usual roost at the end of the bar, where Ben Turner was nursing a Knickerbocker beer. "You were good tonight, Harry. Well, you're always good, but tonight I thought you were exceptional."

"Can the bullshit, Ben. You've got a tin ear and always have."

"What's the latest on the Worthington case?"

"There's nothing new on the Worthington case. I saw the Reed kid. I have that gut feeling that he's in the Tombs on a bum rap. Only gut feelings don't stand up to cross-examinations by District Attorney Timothy Brogan. Maggie's arranged for me to meet the cast of *Detective Fitzroy's Casebook* when they get together tomorrow to start rehearsing their next program. If Reed didn't kill Worthington, someone connected with that show did. Right now I need all the information I can get."

"Maybe you should talk to Ed Sullivan. He's got all the inside dope on the wonderful world of radio. He's probably in his office right now. I've got my car. C'mon."

A few minutes later we pushed open the door of the cubicle of an office off the city room of the *Daily News*, where Ed Sullivan's fingers were flying across the keyboard of a Remington typewriter in a way that would make a professional typist have fits—no pattern, nothing coming even close to the touch-typing method. The little office sounded like a machine-gun firing range as Sullivan hunched over the Remington. Always a stiff and awkwardly moving guy, Sullivan looked like a puppet whose strings were being yanked by someone clumsy. Without looking up or pausing in his assault on the typewriter, he growled, "Can't you guys see there's a Broadway columnist at work here?"

"Actually, I liked your stuff a lot better when you were just a run-of-the-mill sportswriter," I said.

"Screw you, MacNeil, and the little Hebe fart who dragged you off the streets." Suddenly the machine-gun fire stopped and Sullivan spun around in his swivel chair. "How are you, Harry?"

"Great, Ed."

"Okay, that's over with. What do you want?"

"I'm poking around the murder at Radio City."

"Justifiable homicide no matter who bumped Worthington off." He was not a gossip columnist for no reason. "There's no question that concerning radio Worthington was a genius, the guy who wrote the book, a class act professionally. But as a human being? A disaster. One of those people who get a kick out of wielding power over others. Showbiz is full of 'em, as you know."

"Was Worthington a frequent item in your column?"

"Harry, I thought you read my column religiously."

"I may have missed one or two."

"I put the name Derek Worthington in the column from time to time. I write about little old New York and Derek Worthington was a man you ran into around town. He always had a beauty of one kind or another on his arm or on a string. Ordinarily I wouldn't pay much attention to who was out on a date with whom if the person on the arm was a nobody, but Worthington's nobodies often became somebodies. If Derek was squiring a new face, it might mean that person was about to become a star. Worthington made a lot of nobodies into stars. Of course, before he made them stars, he made them. He didn't invent the casting couch, but he raised it to a fine art. I suppose that was a natural consequence of his own past. He got his own start on the casting couch a few years ago. The story is that he got his first job as a radio announcer on Rita DeLong's musical program because

Rita fell in love with another part of his anatomy before she fell in love with his voice box. He soon left the announcing behind him in favor of producing programs and giving himself the starring roles in them. It's all in the files if you want to have a look at them."

I glanced at Ben. "It might be helpful."

Ben knew the look I was giving him. "I'll get a copyboy to dig through the morgue for stuff on Worthington."

"And anything on the others connected with Worthington's programs?"

"Anything for a loyal reader, Harry." Ben chuckled.

"Tell me about this kid they've charged with the murder," Sullivan said. "Did he do it?"

"He says he didn't."

"What do you say?"

"I say he probably didn't."

"Can I print that?"

"Sure, but we'll both look silly if I'm wrong."

"Harry MacNeil wrong? May the saints prevent it."

## 9

The next afternoon when I strolled into Rockefeller Plaza to meet Maggie Skeffington, the Christmas tree was all lights, towering eighty-five feet above a thousand kids gawking upward and clutching the hands of their harried parents while silver skates flashed and shushed on the ice rink below and carols lilted out on loudspeakers tucked behind evergreen streamers and immense wreaths. The official city Christmas tree stood in the park in front of City Hall downtown, but it was a remote and spindling dwarf compared to the leviathan that the Rockefellers erected in the heart of midtown, a colossus that seemed to grow taller every year. The idea for a tree had started with the construction men who propped up an ordinary tree in 1931 and strung a few lights on it to brighten their season of bone-chilling labor when Rockefeller Center was still a mad dream. In 1934 the tree was sixty feet tall and draped with twelve hundred colored lights. In 1935 it was seventy feet high and the lights numbered seventeen hundred. In 1936 it was eighty feet and there were four thousand lights. The Macy's Thanksgiving Day parade heralding the arrival of Santa Claus, whose procession started on Central Park West and ended at Herald Square, may have signaled the gala start of Christmas shopping, but every New Yorker knew that the holiday season didn't really begin until someone threw the switch that turned on the lights of the Rockefeller Center tree in the first week of December. The tree and the annual Christmas stage show at Radio City Music Hall with its living Nativity had become a hallmark of the season of joy in the city of dreams.

In the midst of this festive swirl waited Maggie. She looked alone, tiny and bewildered and completely oblivious to the tree, the stately thrust of the RCA Building, the blur of colors that were sweaters and scarves and stylish skating costumes on the rink, and the tangy smell of decorative evergreens. "It's quite a festive scene, isn't it?" I asked as I came up to her.

She turned and craned her neck to look up at the tree. "I assume from the tone of pride in your voice, Mr. Harry MacNeil, that you're a native New Yorker."

"Born and bred in Brooklyn, actually."

"Well, Brooklyn's New York."

"Not to the people of Brooklyn. Over there the folks think of Manhattan as New York. 'The city,' they call it. It's the same way in the other boroughs. There's

Brooklyn, Queens, the Bronx, and Staten Island; then there's New York. Brooklyn was once a city in its own right, you know. Brooklynites still have that fierce independence. Just mention Brooklyn on the radio and the studio audience bursts into applause. Plus, there's always the Dodgers. I haven't lived in Brooklyn for years and I guess I qualify as a sophisticated Manhattanite, a real New Yorker after all that time, but as the saying goes, you can take the boy out of Brooklyn but you'll never take Brooklyn out of the boy."

She was now looking up the seventy floors of the RCA Building, the jewel of John D. Rockefeller's fabulous gamble. "I hail from a little town in Pennsylvania. I bet there are more people in that skyscraper at this moment than the whole population of my little town." She lowered her head and looked at me sidewise. "You don't know a darned thing about small towns."

"Not much."

She lifted her eyes to the RCA Building again. "Since I was a little kid I dreamed of coming to New York to be on the radio. I don't know how many nights I spent sitting on the floor in front of our big Atwater Kent radio and listening to the programs coming from New York City. I loved *Manhattan Merry-Go-Round*." She closed her eyes. " 'Here's the *Manhattan Merry-Go-Round* that brings you the bright side of life, that whirls you in music to all the big night spots of New York town. . . . ' " She opened her eyes and smiled at me. "Those were seductive words. My first dream was to be a singer on *Manhattan Merry-Go-Round*, but by the time I was in high school the acting bug had bitten and I desired nothing more than to be a radio actress and to star in one of the plays on *First Nighter*. Imagine my shock and disappointment when I arrived in New York and discovered that my favorite dramatic show didn't even come from New York. It originated in Chicago! But that didn't discourage me. There were plenty of shows that did come from New York. I guess I auditioned for all of them. I finally got a small part on *The Goldbergs*." She laughed at herself. "I was awful. Can you imagine this little Protestant girl from a small town trying to be a Jewish girl, complete with Lower East Side accent?"

Listening to her, I could imagine her in almost any role. She was a charmer. Real star quality.

"There I was struggling and certain that I was going to be fired until that wonderful woman Gertrude Berg, who is so wonderful as Molly Goldberg, took me aside and said, 'Listen, darling, just relax and have fun and you'll be just fine.' Later Miss Berg helped me get an audition for *John's Other Wife*. That's a soap opera, in case you didn't know. Then I heard about auditions for the part of Miss Molloy."

"And then you fell in love with David Reed."

"Love at first sight, as they say." Her baby blue eyes got misty. "Now, now—" Big tears started a slow crawl down her apple cheeks. "Oh, Harry, you've got to save him."

"It would be a damned sight easier if David didn't have that history of arguments and fights with Worthington!"

"None of us escaped from clashing with Derek, but neither did any of us leave. We were committed to the program and to Derek in spite of our occasional spats. The police are making too much of those flare-ups between David and Derek."

"What was your relationship to Worthington?"

The flash of her ice blue eyes made it clear that she was offended by the question. "There was no relationship but a professional one." Her eyes narrowed and that defiant chin jutted out. "What gutter story did you hear from Shoemaker?"

"He said you and Worthington had more than a professional relationship."

"That's a lie."

"Worthington apparently was a pretty good practitioner of the casting couch."

"Not with me."

"He never made a pass at you?"

"He made a pass, sure, but he never got beyond that."

"Was that why David took a poke at him in the Rainbow Room?"

She looked away again. She sounded hurt and puzzled. "I don't know what that was about."

"You weren't there?"

"David and Derek had gone to the Rainbow Room together for dinner. I assumed it was to talk about David taking over the Fitzroy role."

"Surely David told you what happened?"

"He told me what happened but he wouldn't tell me why."

"Your boyfriend certainly kept a lot from you, Maggie."

"Yes," she sighed sadly, "and maybe if he hadn't . . ."

I suddenly hugged her. "Cheer up. You've got Harry MacNeil on your side, after all." That seemed to comfort her and I felt pretty good even though I had nothing more than a hunch that Reed was innocent. "Are you hungry, Maggie? I'm famished. Allow me to treat you to the finest meal in New York, a hot dog with mustard and sauerkraut from that little cart at the corner. It's the best food bargain in town, in case you didn't know."

Taking my arm, grinning, she said, "Harry, there's not an actor or actress in this town who hasn't survived for weeks at a time on pushcart hot dogs."

As if to prove her point, she greeted the man behind the cart by name. "Two of your best, Tony." She laughed. "And load on the kraut!"

"Sure thing, Miss Skeffington," said Tony with a nod as he flipped open the lid to his cart.

The smell of the hot dogs scented the cold air.

A line from Gershwin's "They All Laughed" popped into my head as Maggie and I crossed the private street between the sunken plaza where naked Prometheus glittered goldenly under the scintillating branches of the towering Rockefeller Center Christmas tree and the grandeur of the entrance to 30 Rockefeller Plaza. "They all laughed at Rockefeller Center," said the Gershwin lyric, "now they're fighting to get in." The Great Hall, as they called the main lobby, was a jam of visitors, some taking one of the tours of Rockefeller Center and some on their way to or from appointments in the offices stacked above our heads for seventy floors, but most were holiday-happy people come to gawk at the lights on the tree. Beneath their feet was a brass and terrazzo mosaic floor. Around them were the walls of French-gray Vermont marble. All of this was dominated by Jośe Maria Sert's four murals depicting man's intellectual mastery of the worst elements of man's material universe: labor, disease, slavery, and war. There was no panel by the Spanish muralist on the subject of man's oldest plague—murder—yet the sin of Cain had reached us even in a grandiose temple of broadcasting in the heart of Manhattan.

A handsome young man in a blue page's uniform smiled at Maggie and offered a cheery good afternoon as we turned from the main lobby to the bank of elevators reserved for use by the men and women who worked in Radio City. Opposite the elevators a broad red-carpeted stairway led to a mezzanine where the Radio City guided tours formed and ended. It was from the tour mezzanine that Robby Miller had led the group that happened to be passing the slightly ajar door of the control room to Studio 6B at the moment when Derek Worthington had been shot to death by the gun from a sound-effects truck.

Maggie noticed that I was gazing across the Radio City lobby at the tour area. "Have you ever taken the studio tour, Harry?"

"Nope." Touring the broadcasting studios of Radio City was one of those things I'd always planned to do but never had, like taking the boat out to the Statue of Liberty and climbing up into the torch or catching the Christmas show at Radio City Music Hall or going horseback riding in Central Park.

"You should try it. It's very interesting. Now they even include a look at one of NBC's new television studios. David says that's where the future is for drama. He says one day television will be a theater in everybody's living room."

"Don't know if I'd care for that," I muttered as the elevator door slid closed and we began our ascent to the Blue Network studios.

"Why not?"

"Well, what I like about radio is the demands it puts on the imagination. I kind of like having the theater in my mind. I'm not sure I'd want to the have it all laid out for me on a screen."

"You go to the movies, don't you?"

"Not much."

She was laughing as we stepped from the elevator into another lobby, this one festooned with framed photographs of the stars of radio—Jack Benny, Fred Allen, Edgar Bergen and Charlie McCarthy, Fred Waring, and an assortment of faces that I did not recognize but whose voices I was sure were as familiar to me as my own. Along a corridor at intervals between these rows of publicity portraits were windowless gray doors to the studios, where those faces and voices entertained listeners they referred to as the "ladies and gentlemen of the radio audience," whom Walter Winchell, whose face I noted among the portraits, addressed as "Mr. and Mrs. America." Above each door was an electric sign that warned anyone about to venture through whether or not that particular studio was ON THE AIR. Studio 6B's light was off; the studio itself, dim, cool, and vast, was empty except for the equipment needed to make radio work—microphones, the sound-effects truck, music stands for holding scripts, a piano, and the ever-present organ whose trills, riffs, and stabs punctuated and underscored.

Set into the wall a floor above Studio 6B was a rectangle of glass behind which was a dark space I assumed was the control room where a careless engineer had left a mike open and inadvertently allowed the shot that killed Derek Worthington to be heard by those following Robby Miller on his guided tour of the behind-the-scenes wonders of network radio.

Within a few minutes the men and women whose jobs were to turn words on paper into a thrilling episode from *Detective Fitzroy's Casebook* had ambled into Studio 6B. The room bubbled with the precisely articulated, smoothly modulated voices of America's most popular mystery drama.

The voice I recognized immediately belonged to Jason Patrick, who played Fitzroy's sidekick on the program. Sergeant O'Donnell was the kind of partner every real-life cop dreamed of having at his side: shrewd, resourceful, brave, and willing to pitch in and pull his share of the load of legwork and tedious detail that is the lot of the policeman. In the theater of my mind I'd always pictured Sergeant O'Donnell as a Johnny Broderick with smooth edges. The actor who conveyed that image was just the opposite: tall, immaculately tailored in a suit that had Brooks Brothers all over it and an expensive white shirt beneath it, the starched French cuffs extending below the sleeves of the jacket just enough to display gold cuff links with diamonds inset. His long face sported a Douglas Fairbanks moustache. Only the voice belonged to Sergeant O'Donnell. When Maggie introduced us and

I complimented him on his accurate portrayal of a New York City cop, he seemed flattered. "To hear such praise from a genuine detective is quite an honor, but, of course, the character was the invention of Derek Worthington and the words that Sergeant O'Donnell speaks come from the typewriter of our fabulous writer, Veronica Blake." He looked around the studio in search of her, but the writer of *Detective Fitzroy's Casebook* was not in sight. "Veronica's been pressed this week to come up with a script. She's writing us an episode that centers on O'Donnell, you see, with the explanation that Fitzroy is out of town on another case. We're biding time until we find out what will happen to the show. What a tragedy to lose Derek! He was not only a great friend of mine after all these years of working together on *Fitzroy's Casebook*, but also an inspiration."

"That's quite a tribute, Mr. Patrick."

"It's heartfelt, Mr. MacNeil." He paused and glanced at Maggie. "You've undoubtedly heard that Derek was a stern taskmaster. I'd be the last to deny it. He took great pride in the art of radio drama and went far beyond what was required to bring into radio, especially into his own productions, the most promising talent. Young talents like Maggie Skeffington."

"And David Reed?"

"David was one of Derek's protegés. I can't believe— I won't believe—that David murdered Derek."

"I understand they'd been having some difficulties."

Patrick glanced at Maggie again, nervously. When he looked back at me he was forcing a smile. "Has there ever been a friendship, especially a professional friendship, that hasn't had its bumpy moments? The greatest literature of the theater has dealt with the strains upon true friendship."

"What sort of shape was your friendship with Derek in?"

"Ours was one of those friendships that endured so

many strains that it acquired a shell of invulnerability. I am proud to say that Derek and I off the air had exactly the relationship that Fitzroy and O'Donnell have on the air. In the realm of fictional crime there have been two truly great friendships: Holmes and Watson, Fitzroy and O'Donnell. Our fictional bond carried into real life."

Maggie Skeffington was struggling to keep a smile off her face and had to take a step back so Patrick wouldn't notice her amusement. Taking her cue, I asked, "I assume from what you said that you had been making plans to join Derek when he moves to Hollywood to bring Fitzroy to the screen. You were going to play O'Donnell in the movies, I assume?"

"That is an obvious assumption, but Derek was adamant that the quality of the radio broadcasts not suffer from his absence. He asked me, as a favor, to remain with the radio program in New York. I was deeply moved by his confidence."

"Then it didn't bother you that you weren't going to Hollywood?"

"Not in the least," he said with a smile that was pure acting, but that smiling mask slipped a little bit when I suggested that his staying in New York also removed the problem of having to leave the woman he was in love with—Veronica Blake, the writer of *Fitzroy's Casebook*. Startled and caught off guard, he needed a moment to recover his composure. "It hasn't taken you very long to plug into the Radio City gossip mill, Mr. MacNeil." His eyes drifted to Maggie. "Darling, have you been tattling?"

"Actually," I said, "I got that from another source."

"May I ask whom?" he asked, turning back to me with a flash of anger in his eyes.

"Oh, it's not important."

"Veronica and I are hardly an item, Mr. MacNeil," he replied tartly. Turning away, he gave Maggie a withering look and then strode away.

Maggie was suddenly all smiles. "Who'd you get that item from, Harry?"

"Freddy Shoemaker volunteered it. Was he lying or is there something between Patrick and Blake?"

"What if there is? What's it got to do with Derek's murder?"

"Maybe nothing. Except Shoemaker said Derek and Veronica Blake were also, uh, involved."

Maggie shook her head. "Impossible."

"Why's it impossible?"

"I'd've known. The whole cast would have known."

"Do you happen to know where Jason Patrick was at the time of the murder?"

She chewed her lip a moment, thinking, then nodded. "Yes. He was with Veronica in the cafeteria. They were already at a table when Rita and I came in."

"Rita."

"Rita DeLong, our organist. Come. I'll introduce you."

Anyone who had listened to the radio at all in the past few years knew the name Rita DeLong. It appeared in the list of credits at the end of a flock of radio shows from afternoon soap operas to the best dramatic and musical shows on the air in the evenings. "Rita DeLong and her magic fingers," as she was known on her own daily fifteen-minute musical interludes program on station WEAF, was seated at the studio organ whose keyboard she was able to command, coax, tease, or caress into moods ranging from the zany to the threatening. Hers was the talent that gave radio's dramatic, comedic, or romantic moments the seasoning that kept those moments from coming across flat or even a little ridiculous. Musical backgrounds were to radio what Russian dressing was to a turkey sandwich at Lindy's.

"So this is the fellow who is going to demolish the ridiculous case the police have concocted against David," said Rita as she swung away from her keyboard to face

Maggie and me. She clasped my hand in hers. "You've got quite a fan in Maggie, Mr. MacNeil." As effervescent as a samba on her instrument, a tiny woman, middle-aged and trying hard with makeup and hair tint to deny that fact, Rita DeLong flashed one of those toothy smiles that forms deep dimples at the corners of the mouth and crease lines at the eyes, which would have to be dealt with by a face-lift in not too many years. "You must find the murderer, Mr. MacNeil. We can't permit a horrible misunderstanding to come between Maggie and David. I have my heart set on playing the organ at their wedding. Oh, if only he had come to the cafeteria with us that night. That's what comes of foolish lovers' quarrels. But I know you'll save the day, Mr. MacNeil." She reached for Maggie's hand sympathetically, then startled Maggie by kissing it.

The tender and touching moment was interrupted by the dulcet tones of Jason Patrick. "Attention, everybody. Mr. Richards wishes to say something before we begin the rehearsal."

J. William Richards, the owner of the Mellow-Gold Coffee Company and the sponsor of *Detective Fitzroy's Casebook*, said, "It's a sad moment for all of us. We've each suffered a severe loss in the untimely death of Derek Worthington, but I want you all to know that this wonderful program is going to continue. That is my promise to you and to the network." A burst of applause greeted this announcement and seemed to startle the sponsor. "The rights to the program now belong to our dear friend and producer, Miles Flannagan." He gave a little bow in the direction of the red-haired, freckled, elflike figure of Flannagan, wearing a brown-and-white houndstooth jacket, tan slacks, brown riding boots, and a tan turtleneck sweater. He reminded me of pictures I'd seen of Cecil B. deMille, the Hollywood director whose own radio program, *Lux Radio Theater*, was one of the Blue Network's most popular shows. The Monday-night radio adaptations of Hollywood's biggest movies featured movie stars as the leading actors. With his deMille getup, Miles Flannagan was losing no time in stepping into Derek Worthington's shoes now that he'd inherited Worthington's hottest program.

"Now, boys and girls," said Flannagan, clapping his hands, "shall we get down to work?"

Maggie spoke up. "Before we start, I think I ought to introduce someone I've brought with me to today's rehearsal." She turned to me. "This is Harry MacNeil. He's a private detective. He's going to prove that David did not murder Derek."

The cast members applauded again and I felt as if I'd just been declared the winning contestant on Major Bowes's *Amateur Hour*.

"A private eye?"

"Yep."

Veronica Blake's blue mascaraed eyelids did a little curtsy. She was one of those dames who could give a man one look and know everything about him. "I've been working on a concept for a radio program about a private eye. Maybe you can help me with my research." The eyes opened wide. They were see-right-through-you emerald green. "I think I'd like to research you, Mr. MacNeil." She had a battleship-gray jacket draped across her shoulders and an oystershell-white sweater like the one Lana Turner must have been wearing when she was discovered on the soda fountain stool at Schwab's drugstore in Hollywood. In the crook of her arm she held a thatch of scripts. "Would you like a copy? Since you'll be sitting in during the read-through, a script might keep you from getting lost." She handed me one. "Of course, this is a first draft. There'll be changes before we go on the air Sunday night. You are going to stay around?"

"I expect so."

"Good. You can tell me all about the private eye business and about yourself."

When they had been handed scripts, the cast and crew of *Detective Fitzroy's Casebook* gathered around a table at the center of the studio. At one end sat Veronica Blake, half a dozen pencils and a note pad at the ready for whatever changes the first rehearsal might indicate were required in her script. At the other end, Miles Flannagan presided. For my benefit he went around the table making introductions. To his left sat Jason Patrick, who as Sergeant O'Donnell would have to solve this week's crime solo. Next to him was Maggie. Beside Maggie was an actor named Ben Loman, who would be playing a character named Carson. "Ben," explained Flannagan, "is one of the best character actors in the business, but he was not in the cast on the night of the murder, so you can rule him out as a suspect, Mr. MacNeil."

"Oh, damn," sighed Ben Loman, the voice a remarkable imitation of Jimmy Cagney in *Public Enemy*, "I wanted to be a suspect!"

Across the table from Loman sat Sheila Fay, a brassy-haired and busty actress whose part called for her to be the distraught wife of the man who was murdered in "The Case of the Black Widow," the title of Veronica Blake's latest efforts at the typewriter. "Am I a suspect, Mr. MacNeil?" she asked. "I was in the fateful show."

"Sheila and I were having coffee in the cafeteria at the time of Derek's murder," said the next actor at the table, Bart Mason, a regular on the show in many roles.

This week he was a heavy named Drake. His voice was surprisingly ballsy for a guy whose mannerisms were decidedly effeminate.

Next to Mason sat a guy who looked like a longshoreman. His name was Jerry Nolan and he was the sound-effects man. "I know you'll have to talk to me, Mr. MacNeil. You'll want to know what the cops wanted to know. How did my pistol get to be a murder weapon? Well, anybody could have gotten to that gun while we were on break before air time, so—"

"Yes, plenty of time for that later," interrupted Miles Flannagan. "Right now we have a show to rehearse." The last person to be introduced was Guff Taylor, the technician who had left on the microphone that picked up the sound of the shot and thereby removed any question as to the time of the murder.

As those around the table began work on the script, the show's sponsor, a benign smile on his face, edged toward the studio door and a discreet exit. I caught up with him in the hallway. "Mr. Richards, I wonder if I might ask you a few questions?"

The owner of the Mellow-Gold Coffee Company seemed upset at the prospect. "I disapprove of your getting mixed up in this awful affair, sir. There's been enough bad publicity as it is."

"I appreciate the delicacy of your position, Mr. Richards, but I'm sure you don't want an innocent man to go to the chair."

"All I want is for this to blow over."

"I understand that Derek Worthington and you were good friends as well as partners in radio. I know you want his killer caught and punished."

"I really don't see how I can be of any help to you, Mr. MacNeil."

"Well, sir, it's like Detective Fitzroy says on your program. 'Solving crime is the same as putting together a jigsaw puzzle. You've got to have *all* the pieces.'"

"I had no idea you were a fan of *Fitzroy's Casebook*, Mr. MacNeil," he said with a pleased smile.

"I'm just like everybody else in the country, Mr. Richards—glued to the radio Sunday nights. And, if it will get you to trust me and to help me, I want you to know that I start off every day with a cup of Mellow-Gold."

The sponsor laughed. "You're an Irishman, aren't you, Mr. MacNeil? Full of blarney."

"I'm just searching for all the pieces to the jigsaw puzzle, Mr. Richards. Who knows, maybe you've got the one piece that will make sense of it?"

"We can talk in the cafeteria just down the hall, but stay away from the coffee. It isn't Mellow-Gold and it tastes like cat piss." The cafeteria where everyone in the cast of *Detective Fitzroy's Casebook*—except the victim and the young man accused of his murder—had been at the time of the murder was a crowded room dotted with functional tables and chairs and decorated with more publicity photos of the stars of radio. Avoiding the cat's piss coffee, J. William Richards and I sipped Cokes at a table in a corner beneath a portrait of a glowering Arturo Toscanini, maestro of the NBC Symphony Orchestra. "My advertising agency people tell me that the murder might be the best thing that could have happened to the show I sponsor," said Richards as he slowly turned his glass of Coke between pudgy fingers, "but I don't go along with those who say publicity is publicity and it's all good as long as they spell your name correctly. The last thing I'd want is a big jump in our Crosley ratings as a result of Derek being murdered. For a couple of days I thought about dropping my sponsorship of the show. Then Miles Flannagan came to my office and we had a long talk and I agreed to stay with the show. Miles is a good man and I know he'll maintain the high standards of *Detective Fitzroy's Casebook* now that he owns the show himself. I always thought Derek owned it outright but

Miles brought an agreement with him when he came to see me that showed that the show is now his. Well, even though I had qualms about continuing as the sponsor, I didn't want to have to hurt the folks who had worked so hard on the show for so long. After my talk with Miles I called the network and told them I wanted to continue to sponsor the show as long as they intended to keep it on the air. In some ways I expect it will be a better show with Miles at the helm."

"Is that so? What makes you think that?"

"Oh, it's just the difference in styles. Miles isn't the tyrant that Derek was. I happen to be one of those businessmen who believes it's good policy to have happy people working for you. Mellow-Gold Coffee opened its doors to the unions long before other companies were forced into it. There's never been any labor trouble in my company, sir, and there never will be. If you treat people decently, they'll work harder for you. Miles shares that philosophy."

"Derek was a bit of a slave driver, wasn't he?"

The owner of Mellow-Gold Coffee sipped his Coke. "Derek had a mean streak in him, no doubt. I don't know why. He just seemed to derive pleasure out of being hard. We had quite a few heart-to-heart chats on the subject but he couldn't change. That was his personality. We saw things differently. That's what makes horse races, eh?"

"On the whole, though, you were happy with what Worthington delivered on your behalf?"

"We did well every week in the Crosleys and those ratings points translated into sales in the grocery stores. Selling coffee is what I do, after all. Derek left the coffee business to me and I left the radio business to him."

"In case it matters, Mr. Richards, I think your way's the best. I never believed in kicking people around either. Too bad Derek Worthington didn't take your advice. If he had he might be alive today."

"Derek never took anyone's advice. He marched to

his own drum. I was very much against his plan to leave the program to go to Hollywood. We argued heatedly. I'm telling you this because you will probably hear it from someone else. Lest you think our difference over his leaving for Hollywood was a reason for me to wish to stop him and no matter the cost, I want you to understand that as much as I wished Derek to remain in New York there were limits to my opposition to his plan to leave."

"Where were you at the time he was murdered?"

"Between the end of the rehearsal, which was just before six o'clock, and air time I was in conference with Miles Flannagan in Miles's office. That was until a couple of minutes before seven."

"At which time you returned to the studio?"

"I returned to the control room. I always watch the broadcast from the control room."

"So, when you left Derek's office you returned to the control room and that's when you learned that Derek had been shot?"

"Not immediately. It was only when we noticed the hubbub in the studio that we realized something was amiss."

"You said 'when we noticed' the hubbub?"

"Guff Taylor and I. He was in the control room. We chatted a little before we noticed that something was wrong in the studio. That's how we learned that Derek had been shot."

"There's a big window looking down into the studio. You didn't see Derek lying there?"

"You couldn't see the body just by glancing through the window. It lay close to the wall almost directly down from the window. No, only when the others came in and discovered the body did Guff and I realize what had happened."

"How long were you and Guff chatting before the others came into the studio?"

"Several minutes. I didn't pay attention. Guff was

preparing for the broadcast and I was just sitting in my customary chair, and then he noticed the unusual activity below. He'd been putting things in order. Guff is a very orderly person, you see. I suppose you have to have that kind of orderly mind to be as good as he is at his job. He was straightening up the racks of transcriptions and making sure his script was in the right order and then Guff noticed the hubbub in the studio and turned on the talk-back system to ask what was the matter. It was at that moment that Guff and I found out that Derek had been lying there dead below the control room window the whole time. It was a terrible shock."

"Do you remember who was in the studio at that time?"

"Everyone except David Reed. He came into the studio a minute or two later."

"Do you believe he killed Derek?"

"It must have been him. He was the only one who could not verify his whereabouts at the time of the murder, but what do I know about murder? I'm a coffee maker. All I know about crime is what I hear on *Detective Fitzroy's Casebook*."

12

When I returned to Studio 6B the talents that gave America its most popular detective show had moved away from the table to the microphones. Quietly, I edged past the knot of actors reading the lines from Veronica Blake's script in the voices of the characters assigned to them and approached the sprawl of machinery—tables piled with everything from coconut shells to crumpled balls of cellophane, a full-sized door hung on a wheeled frame, a Chinese gong, and something that looked like a waterwheel—that was the domain of sound-effects man Jerry Nolan. Immediately I noticed that he had gotten himself a .38-caliber Smith and Wesson pistol to replace the one Lt. Bill Tinney had impounded as evidence in the murder of Derek Worthington. Jerry Nolan gave me a smile and a wink as he waited for a cue to provide the sound effects of the scene on the next page of Veronica's script.

"When I got to the widow's house," said Jason Patrick as Sergeant O'Donnell, "it was raining cats and dogs."

Jerry Nolan produced the rain by turning the waterwheel contraption at his side. Slowly spinning the wheel, he let a torrent of rice pour from his other hand, the kernels spilling onto the turning wheel and cascading from it to a thin sheet of tin. The effect was the sound of rain on a roof.

"The widow came to the door," said Sergeant O'Donnell.

Jerry Nolan let the rain machine spin to a stop as he reached behind him to open the door.

"It's you, Sergeant," said Sheila Fay as the widow. "Come in."

Nolan closed the door.

"Her house was cozy and warm," said Sergeant O'Donnell, "and the widow showed me to the library."

The sound-effects man snatched up a ball of cellophane and, holding it close to a microphone and gently squeezing it, created the sound of a crackling fire.

"We sat by the fireplace," said Sergeant O'Donnell.

"No, wait!" Miles Flannagan's voice boomed through a loudspeaker beneath the window of the control room one floor above the studio. "The scene is all wrong. Let's take a half-hour break while Veronica and I work on it."

Jerry Nolan put down his cellophane and gave me an impish smile. "Sometimes I feel like a one-handed paper-hanger, Mr. MacNeil."

"I guess you have something in all this stuff that will create any kind of sound."

"Well, sometimes it's simpler just to put on a sound-effects record. For instance, nobody's found a way yet to reproduce the sound of an airplane. Or the motor of an automobile. I use recordings for sounds like those."

Gingerly, I picked up the Smith and Wesson. "But when you need a gunshot you fire a real pistol?"

"Right off the assembly line."

"How come you left a real pistol lying around the studio that night?"

"To save time when I came back for the broadcast. I always leave my equipment set up between the dress rehearsal and the broadcast. You see, I was doing sound effects for another show at the time. I had exactly two minutes to get from that studio to this one. There just wouldn't've been enough time to unpack the gear. It's a routine I've been following for years."

"A routine that someone knew well."

"David Reed knew the routine, Mr. MacNeil."

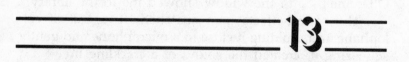

Except for Miles Flannagan and Veronica Blake, who were huddled together and going over the script's unworkable scene behind the glass of the control room one floor up, the cast of the show drifted down the corridor to the cafeteria. Maggie ordered a cup of coffee, apparently never having heard her sponsor's opinion of it. I picked up another Coke. We sat near the door beneath a photograph of Kay Kyser, whose *Kollege of Musical Knowledge* had made the band leader's southern accent as famous as his band's theme song, "Thinking of You." The photo showed "The Old Professor" in a graduation cap and gown leaning close enough to an NBC microphone to kiss it. "What did you and Mr. Richards talk about?"

I smiled. "You noticed us sneak away."

"The whole cast noticed."

"J. William Richards is quite a fellow. Very loyal."

"None of us had any doubt that he would stick by us."

"Miles Flannagan had his doubts. He begged Richards not to drop his sponsorship. Of course, Flannagan had more than a job at stake. Did you know that Flannagan has inherited the ownership of *Fitzroy's Casebook?*" The surprised look on her face gave me my answer. "Becoming the sole owner of a successful radio series seems like a pretty good motive for murder. It's certainly stronger than the one David Reed had. Wouldn't you agree?"

"The problem is, Miles has an alibi just like everybody else."

"Everybody but David."

"You still believe it was possible for David to have killed Derek, don't you?"

"He's the only one without that alibi."

"The killer might be someone not connected with the show."

"The killer had to know the show inside and out, Maggie."

"Someone who'd *been* on the show? What about Shoemaker?"

"He was making a movie at the time." I hadn't personally checked out that angle, but I was certain that

Shoemaker was telling the truth. As much as I'd've liked to hang the Worthington murder around Shoemaker's scrawny neck, I knew that was a pipe dream. "It's quite a case. One worthy of Detective Fitzroy. Plenty of people with motives. Derek managed to put together quite a roster of folks who hated him, in varying degrees, but David's the one who was angry enough to get into a public altercation with Derek."

"David was just disappointed because he wasn't going to get the Fitzroy part."

"I think there was more to it than that."

"Such as what?"

"Such as Derek getting fresh with you?"

"That's ridiculous."

"Then there must have been something else, something that David wouldn't even tell you about." She didn't want to hear it.

"There seem to be a lot of people who were upset at not being invited to go along with Worthington to California," she said.

"California?" said a familiar voice behind me, "California is okay if you're an orange." Maggie exploded with laughter as I turned to look up into a hound-dog face from which squeaked the twangy nasal voice of Fred Allen. He looked past me at laughing Maggie. "Stay in New York, darling, you'd look lousy in sunglasses." The comedian turned his eyes toward me. "Is this man an agent?"

"No," laughed Maggie. "He's a private detective."

"Oh, well, that's okay. I've warned you about agents, Maggie." The twinkling eyes above bags that would have made a bloodhound envious shifted from Maggie back to me. He put a hand on my shoulder. "I'm sorry if I insulted you, mister. There are two kinds of people a gal like Maggie has to watch out for. Agents and network executives. Now take that fellow in the corner over there." The eyes darted toward a young man in a double-breasted pinstripe suit. "He's one of the senior executives at Radio City. He has a whole staff of network junior executives who report to him. He's very good at his job. Do you know why?"

"Why, Mr. Allen?"

The comedian's craggy face lit up. "You're a wonderful straight man, Mr., uh—"

"MacNeil."

"Well, Mr. MacNeil, I'll tell you why that executive is so good at being the boss of other network executives. You see, when he was at Yale he was an all-American quarterback. You know when a quarterback stands behind the line when the linemen bend over, he is looking at a bunch of assholes. So when that fellow calls a meeting, he is doing the same thing, and he's happy." Pausing, deadpan, he waited for Maggie and me to stop laughing, then added, "When that fellow comes to the office at nine o'clock in the morning he finds a molehill on his desk. It's his job to make a mountain out of it by five o'clock." When the laughter subsided again he looked at Maggie once more. "Stay in New York, darling Maggie. Forget the West Coast. You can take all the sincerity in Hollywood, put it in a flea's navel, and have room left over for three caraway seeds and an agent's heart." With that he strolled away toward the food line.

"I have a feeling we just witnessed the rehearsal for his show tonight." I chuckled.

"Oh, Fred's always like that. The jokes just roll off his lips. He's probably the best writer in radio. As to California, he truly hates it. He and his wife, Portland, like New York and live in a small apartment at Fifty-eight and Ninth."

"He seems to like you a lot."

"Fred likes everybody. In fact, he's a soft touch through and through. Can't resist helping someone who's down on his luck. They line up on Forty-ninth Street after his radio show with their hands out. He hands out dollar bills. Even Rockefeller only gave out dimes." She was looking across the cafeteria admiringly at Fred Allen. "He keeps asking me to be on his show."

"Why haven't you accepted?"

"Derek didn't permit his regular cast members to work on other shows."

"That was damned selfish."

"Anyway, Fred's show's schedule and ours conflict. He's rehearsing now for his broadcast tonight, and as you know, we're rehearsing, too. When this trouble involving David is over maybe I'll give some serious thought to Mr. Allen's offer." Suddenly she brightened, her pretty face lighting up. "I'm very good at comedy, Harry."

The rest of the cast who had been taking their break in the cafeteria were starting to drift back toward Studio 6B. I decided to go up to the control room to have a chat with the lanky, curly-haired young man who was the engineer, who'd left a mike switch on and provided a crowd of witnesses to the shot that killed Derek Worthington.

# 14

Tilted back in a chair with his hands folded across his flat belly, Guff Taylor was staring at a huge clock whose red second hand was clicking off the moments while Miles Flannagan gave his cast script changes in the studio below. Like almost everyone I'd met in the radio business, Taylor was young. He had a loosened bow tie and rolled-up shirt sleeves, and he kept his eyes on the clock as if he expected it to miss a tick or stop altogether. In front of him spread the slanting facade of a control console that looked like an overturned gray bathtub except for the rows of switches, control knobs that resembled inverted cooking pots, and push buttons surrounding a meter whose needle bounced every time Miles Flannagan said something in the studio. To Taylor's left stood a pair of turntables with storage bins beneath them, their vertical slots packed with large record discs in paper sleeves. Along the wall behind him were similar turntables. "This is pretty impressive," I said. "Looks like something straight out of Buck Rogers."

"Not so complicated." He looked at me sidewise. "So you're the private eye Maggie hired."

"Harry MacNeil." I held out my hand.

"Guff Taylor." His handshake was tight as a vise.

"That's an unusual name."

He smiled a little. "I'm said to have a reputation for not taking any guff."

"That's a fine reputation to have."

He turned and looked at me directly. "I've heard that you don't take any guff either." I shrugged and smiled noncommittally. "I assume you're going to ask me about the infamous open mike."

"Well, it was that open mike that made it possible to know the exact time of Derek Worthington's death."

"Yeah, well, nobody's perfect."

I nodded at the clusters of switches on the control panel. "If I had your job I'd probably be always leaving something on." I swept my eyes around the control room. "It all looks pretty bewildering to me."

Taylor shook his head. "Don't be cute, Mr. MacNeil. If you want to know about this equipment, ask."

"I see why that nickname stuck to you. Sure I would like to know about all this. I'm cursed with curiosity. I guess that's why I'm a detective."

Deftly and with a minimum of words he explained the control room to me, the workings of the panel with its switches, knobs, and buttons. The turntables to his left were for playing records, the ones against the wall for making them. "We call it cutting." He bent down and pulled out one of the large discs stored beneath the playback machines. "We cut what we call ETs. That's short for 'electrical transcription.' We can record fifteen minutes on each side of these sixteen-inch babies. They're made of a base of glass or metal with a special coating that those recording arms with their special needles cut the grooves into. So when you hear an announcer say that such and such a show is transcribed, it's one of these spinning on a turntable that you're hearing on your radio. Are you a fan of *Detective Fitzroy's Casebook*, Mr. Mac-Neil?"

"Sure am."

"Then I'm sure you know if the program is transcribed or what we call live."

I chuckled. "Afraid I don't."

Taylor shook his head. "Nobody can know, but you could never convince Derek of that. He had this crazy idea that the radio audience could spot the difference between a transcribed show and a live one. As a result we were always live."

"If that's the case, what did you do the night Derek was murdered? You couldn't've been live with the star dead and the announcer under arrest. Was the broadcast canceled?"

"Luckily Miles Flannagan always had me transcribe the dress rehearsals. Since Derek was shot after the rehearsal, we had the program on ET. That's what went on the air that night."

"Jerry Nolan thinks you can detect the difference between a recorded gunshot and a real one."

"That's bullshit. Pardon my French. I've been cutting discs for a long time and I challenge anyone to tell me what the difference is. There's no difference at all. Today's recording techniques are so perfected that no one can know. In fact, transcriptions are so good that if a show is on an ET it has to be identified as such. I'm sure you've heard an announcer say 'transcribed' or 'by transcription' often enough. Derek never wanted that said of his shows. He wanted the audience to know what they were hearing was direct from the studio. Frankly, it was a pain in the ass because of the repeat for the West Coast. Do you know about repeats for the West Coast, Mr. MacNeil?" I shrugged and grinned my ignorance. "Because of the time difference between here and California we always repeated *Fitzroy's Casebook* three hours later so it would be on the air at the same time on the West Coast as here. Likewise, if a show is on the air here in New York at seven o'clock in the evening and it's a live broadcast originating in Hollywood, they have to do it at four in the afternoon out there and then do it again at seven for the West Coast. Got it?"

"Got it."

"It made for a long day for us on the program because we never got out of here until after the repeat for the West Coast. Just because Derek didn't believe in recordings. It was a crazy prejudice. Someday everything in radio will be recorded. They're making great progress in perfecting new techniques, such as wire recording. I happen to know that engineers are also working on a process that will permit recording on magnetic tape. Mark my words, Mr. MacNeil, what's on one of these sixteen-inch ETs you'll be able to hold in the palm of your hand. That's where I hope my future career will be. Derek was going to help me get a job with RCA Victor's recording studios down in Camden, New Jersey. There's a real challenge in recording music. Are you a music fan, Mr. MacNeil?"

"Of sorts."

"Let me guess." He ran his eyes up and down me.

"Definitely not the classical type." He squinted, thinking. "I'd bet that you're an aficionado of jazz."

"Bingo. How'd you come to that conclusion?"

"You're obviously a guy who has to hang out where the action is. You're a night person. Night people hang out in the clubs. Forgive me for the insult, but you're not exactly the El Morocco type." He stood up to peer over his control panel into the studio below. "The first thing to do if you want to be a successful radio engineer, Mr. MacNeil, is eyeball the studio and make sure all the mikes are plugged in."

"What about making sure the mikes are turned off when the show's over?"

He made a face that indicated he did not appreciate my remark. "That, too."

"Of course, if you hadn't left that mike on we wouldn't know the exact time of the murder."

"I guess so."

"Was there anything else amiss in here when you came back to get ready to go on the air?"

"Such as what?"

I shrugged. "Chairs where they weren't supposed to be? Lights on or off, whichever way you left them?"

"Off. I turned 'em off when I left and they were off when I came back."

"With the lights off in this control room you couldn't see into it from the studio down there, is that right?"

"Correct. The glass becomes like one big mirror."

"With the lights out anybody could have been up here and Derek wouldn't't've known it if he happened to glance up this way."

Guff turned with a quizzical look. "Are you suggesting that someone was in here after I left?"

"How else to explain the open mike switch if you didn't leave it on?"

"I'm a very thorough engineer."

-74-

"There was nothing else out of the ordinary when you returned?"

"Nope."

"How about these record turntables?"

"They were off. That I am sure of. They were off when I left and they were off when I came back." He stood again and crossed the control room to the recording machinery. From the rack of blanks he took down two discs and carefully placed them on the recording turntables. "Did you hear that Miles has changed the policy on transcribing the broadcast?"

"I didn't, no. That ought to make life easier for everyone. Except you, of course. That's one more job for you to handle."

"This? It's a breeze." He was using a soft white cloth to clean the mirrored surfaces of the discs. "The only tricky part is when we have to switch from one to the other, but that's marked on the script, so even that's no big deal."

"You use two transcription discs?"

"Well, you can't very well flip them, either when you're transcribing the show or playing it back. You just segue from one to the other."

"Seems like a waste of recording surface, using only one side each time."

"Well, that's the way it's done."

"Sounds complicated. I'd screw it up if I had to do it."

"Oh, it's not that tricky. Anybody can do it with a little practice."

## 15

After the rehearsal for "The Case of the Black Widow" ended at six o'clock, to make room in the studio for another program, I was waiting for an elevator with Maggie when Veronica Blake turned the corner and hurried over to us. She snaked her arm around mine. "Maggie, I hope you don't have any plans to monopolize Mr. MacNeil this evening because I have some research to do!"

Cattily, Maggie asked, "What sort of research, Veronica?"

"Why, for my new private eye program. Be a dear and lend Mr. MacNeil to me. Do, and I promise to write a part in the new program for you. You can be the private eye's Gal Friday."

The elevator came and Maggie stepped into it. As the door slid closed she made a face. "I don't choose to be typecast, Veronica!"

"Well," chirped Veronica, "here we are alone."

There was, I was sure, more than research into the life of a private eye that Veronica Blake had on her mind. I generally knew when I was being set up to be pumped for information. There was no question about Veronica's motives. She wanted to find out what I'd turned up in my investigation of the Worthington murder in general and what I'd found out about her in particular. Because I usually got more out of the person trying to pump me than that person ever got out of me I went along with her. "Suppose we go up to the Rainbow Grill for a drink?"

"I have a better idea. Let's start with a drink at my place, then I'll change into something more suitable and we'll go out and do the town. A few more drinks in some of the clubs, a nice dinner somewhere, and then dancing at the Rainbow Room. You can teach me everything I ought to know about the detective business."

Veronica Blake was a gal with a Stork Club taste, so it would be an expensive evening, and while my taking her out would be business, I didn't see how I could pass on those expenses to whoever got my bill for investigating the murder of Derek Worthington. Also, there was a chance that it would be a waste of time as well as money. I had to leave open the possibility that Veronica Blake, with all of her come-on looks and words, knew nothing that might shed any light on the case; still, I'd been planning to visit the Rainbow Room to look into that fracas between David Reed and Derek Worthington, and I did have to have dinner, and a few drinks before in some of my usual haunts would not be unusual for me, so I took her up on her plan.

It didn't take her long to get out of her battleship-gray suit and into something in blue and gold, what *Vogue* would have called an evening ensemble. Over the blue and gold she wore a mink jacket. I felt decidedly underdressed in my blue serge evening suit, but she allowed with a laugh and a toss of her long brown hair that I looked just fine. She lived on East Fifty-third Street just a few doors from the Stork Club, so we started out with drinks in the Cub Room. Table fifty was, as usual, reserved for Walter Winchell, but the former song-and-dance man, as Ben Turner liked to refer to Winchell, was not at the table. Sherman Billingsley, Winchell's buddy and owner of the Stork, gave his finger-against-his-nose sign to the headwaiter that Veronica and I were suitable for being seated, and we were shown to a table in the rear that was set aside for customers who were there for drinks rather than a meal. Veronica ordered a champagne cocktail. I had Scotch neat. She asked a few questions about my work and I answered them truthfully. Even to me they sounded dull. "I'm afraid your average private eye isn't the stuff for a weekly radio drama," I said, half-amused, half-apologetically. "We thrive mostly on divorce cases. The last murder I investigated was almost five years ago."

Her eyes lit up. "Tell me about it."

"A two-bit punk named Seldes was gunned down in the Onyx Club. He'd been mixed up in a diamond heist and some hoods bumped him off."

"I'd like to hear more about that case."

"It was in the papers. You could look it up."

She laughed. "Mr. MacNeil, are you really that modest?"

"It's just that with me it's the case I'm working on that matters, not old ones. I was never good at history."

"Very well," she said, taking a sip of her champagne, "tell me about this case."

"You know as much about it as I do." I smiled a little. "Maybe you know more than I do."

"I didn't kill poor Derek, I promise you."

"I've heard from a lot of people who knew Derek who don't seem very upset that he's dead. He seems to have been a rat."

"Derek didn't treat people very well. I suppose it's okay to call him a rat."

"I can't imagine him treating you badly."

She laughed a little, bitterly. "I got my share of the Derek Worthington treatment." She shook her head. "It's hard for me to believe it now, but once I was in love with him. That was the great hidden danger concerning Derek. When you first met him he was charming, oh, so charming, and you just fell in love with him. Somewhere along the line you'd discover that someone else had fallen in love with him and the Derek Worthington charm was being pointed in that person's direction, leaving you out in the cold. Soon after you started noticing the slights, the little cruelties, the calls not returned, the cold shoulder. If you were important to him professionally, he didn't cut you off entirely, but there came the moment when you knew that there was nothing personal in the relationship anymore. This town is littered with Derek's castoffs."

"Why do they—why did you—put up with it?"

"Because when it came to radio Derek was a genius and those who were admitted into his little repertory company became the stars of the business. I know several of Derek's old flames who are now movie stars. They wouldn't have succeeded if he hadn't given them their first break on his radio shows. A Derek Worthington show was an easy way to get to Hollywood. Finally, Derek was on the verge of going to Hollywood himself. It's sad, really, that someone killed him before he got his big chance to take Hollywood by storm the way he took radio."

"It's amazing that everyone I've met had very good reasons to hate Derek's guts, yet they all speak of him with awe."

"Not only awe, Harry. Some will speak of him with love. That's the way things went with Derek. It was love and hate. You didn't know him. If you had, you'd find it easier to understand. He was quite dashing. Handsome in a Robert Taylor kind of way. He'd been an athlete in his youth and always stayed in trim. He was handsome and he was imposing in his size. He was well over six feet tall. Shoulders out to here. He could have become a matinee idol out in Hollywood. It was quite easy to fall in love with Derek, and if he fell in love with you, well, there was no honor greater than that, nothing more flattering, nothing more useful. When he fell out of love with you, that was that. If you fell out of love with him, he was unforgiving. He could cut you off in the wink of an eye and it would be as if you had never existed. Or, if it suited him, he would keep you around and turn that into an even more exquisite punishment."

"Is that why he didn't fire David Reed after Reed threw a punch at him in the Rainbow Room?"

"It's possible. Derek could have fired David, of

course, but he was certainly capable of getting revenge another way, by not giving David the Fitzroy part. That would have been a terrible way to get revenge if you think about it. David would go on being just the show's announcer, while one of Derek's new discoveries played Fitzroy." She lifted the champagne in a toast. "To Derek the rat."

"Was there anyone on the show who didn't get kicked in the teeth by Derek the rat?"

Veronica paused, thinking, then shook her head. "Even darling Rita was stung a few years ago. We all felt Derek's wrath eventually."

"Including Jason Patrick?"

"Ah, I wondered how long you'd take to get around to the relationship between Jason and me."

"Who mentioned a relationship?"

"You did with that know-it-all-detective look in your eyes."

"There's one theory that Jason Patrick hated Derek because he was jealous of Derek's attentions to you."

"Whatever there was between Derek and me was over a long time before he was murdered. Derek had drifted into a new love affair."

"With whom?"

"I don't know, but I sort of expected the new love to turn up playing a role in one of Derek's shows. We'll never know who was the new flame."

"But it was definitely over between you and Derek?"

"Definitely."

"And Jason Patrick knew it was over?"

"Yes." She suddenly smiled. "Does Jason know that you regard him as a suspect?"

"How could he be a suspect? He was in the cafeteria with everyone else at the time of the murder."

"Yes. It's damned unfortunate for Reed that everybody can account for his whereabouts at six-oh-five P.M. Jerry Nolan was working the sound effects on another show. Half of America was witness to Jerry Nolan's whereabouts, thanks to radio. Guff Taylor was in the engineers' lounge and can prove it. Miles Flannagan was with the show's sponsor in Miles's office. And everyone else was in the cafeteria. Except David Reed."

I forced a smile. "You're the expert mystery writer, Veronica. You tell me who done it."

A honey-throated singer with the Ben Cutler orchestra was caressing the lyrics of Johnny Mercer's "Too Marvelous for Words" when Veronica and I picked our way around the edge of the dance floor in the Rainbow Room sixty-five floors above what the room's press agent described as a twinkling carpet of New York's night-lights. There never was a room more elegant than this one with its background of aubergine satin, flashing mirrors, jade-green leather chairs, and emerald-green carpeting below a glittering crystal chandelier suspended from a dome in the ceiling two stories high, where a kaleidoscope of colored lights changed in keeping with the mood of the room's orchestras. There were always two bands on the bill at the Rainbow Room. The other one sharing the honors with Ben Cutler was Eddie LeBaron's rumba band. For those who wished to dance cheek to cheek to the Cutler rhythms or to the bump and bounce of a Latin beat, formal dress was required. The dance floor underfoot was a revolving one.

Veronica Blake smelled of gardenia perfume, ordered

Maine lobster and French wine, and passed up dessert. She wanted to talk about everything but her ideas for a private detective show and the murder of Derek Worthington. Her preferred subject was us. She was a woman on the make and I did nothing to talk her out of it. When she finally went to the powder room I got my chance to talk to the headwaiter about the recent public unpleasantness involving Reed and Worthington.

"The gentlemen were at table thirty. They apparently had much to talk about." He spoke with a French accent and tugged nervously at his white tie. "It was a long time before they were ready to order. I had a sense that it was a conversation of the most personal nature. I have been observing table talk for many years, Mr. MacNeil, and I have a keen sense—without overhearing anything, of course—for what is being discussed. You can immediately recognize business conversations and you can see when the talk is on a more intimate plane. Eventually they raised their voices and I had to admonish them. A few minutes later the violence erupted. Naturally, I asked them to leave and they did, but not together."

"I'd like to talk to the waiter who was taking care of table thirty that evening."

"That would be Pierre, who is not working this evening. I'm sorry. However, I assure you that Pierre would tell you what I have told you. Pierre does not eavesdrop on conversations either. If you wish to know what was said, I suggest that you speak to the young man about it."

When Veronica returned from the powder room the band was playing music that most people favor in the wee hours when the city is drifting from roar to hum. In keeping with the tempo there was a romantic glow in Veronica's eyes. If I had had on the proper suit she would have been content to sway in my arms on the Rainbow Room dance floor until closing time, but in the small hours of night I preferred the sounds that you found on Swing Street, so I persuaded the lady to leave. We walked to Fifty-second Street and started out at the Famous Door. The Door had started something new for Swing Street by bringing in big bands like Woody Herman, Charley Barnet, Teddy Powell, and Count Basie. The Herman big band sound that night was okay, but I still preferred the smaller groups with their purer jazz, so Veronica and I wound up at the Onyx in time for one of its legendary just-before-closing jam sessions. She got quite a kick out of me taking a turn on the clarinet before we strolled from the Onyx back to her apartment on East Fifty-third.

"Everyone in this town seems to know you," she observed as she poured Scotches.

"I've been around."

She sat beside me. The lights were dim, the gardenia perfume was heady, and the lady was still on the make. I was tired and showed it. "You look a little used," she whispered.

"Used," I said, reaching for her, "but not used up."

## 17

I left Veronica sleeping at eight o'clock the next morning and made my way to the Automat at Radio City for coffee and donuts and the morning papers. They were crammed with Christmas advertising, but between the cheery temptations of the season sprawled the sordid details of the follies and felonies of the people of the town Mark Hellinger liked to call "the naked city." The previous afternoon the love-sick paymaster of an ink company had shot and killed a woman Comptometer operator during the company's Christmas party, thus putting a damper on the seasonal jollity. On the brighter side, a couple of hundred business women of the Carroll Club had thrown a party for underprivileged East Side kids. Postmaster General Jim Farley was imploring Americans to wrap their gifts well and mail early for Christmas, although anyone who hadn't mailed by then would need a miracle to get the package delivered by December 25. On the sports pages, Byron Nelson was the leader in the Miami Open golf tournament. The New York Rangers had outskated the Canadiens 4–2 in ice hockey. In the frozen expanses of Finland the Russians were still battering the Finns at the Mannerheim line around Summa, but in Europe the war against the Nazis still had not produced any battles to speak of since war had been declared in September, an uneasy quiet that the radio commentators were scornfully calling the "Sitzkrieg." There was plenty of warfare at sea, however. The Allies were losing dozens of ships and hundreds of thousands of tons of matériel to U-boats not very far off the shores of Long Island. There was nothing in the papers about the murder of Derek Worthington. Nothing is as dead to a newspaper as a week-old murder case that appears to be open and shut.

My gloom and that of the cold morning were brightened a little by the lights on the Rockefeller Center Christmas tree when I turned onto the plaza heading for Radio City. It was time to have a chat with Robby Miller, the tour guide whose punctuality in carrying out his duties permitted the moment of Derek Worthington's death to be set so precisely. Already, as I crossed the street toward the plaza entrance of the RCA Building, there was a crowd around the tree and along the walls above the sunken ice rink where, even at that early hour, skaters were doing their stuff, every girl as pert and graceful as Sonja Henie and every boy as nimble as a Fred Astaire on skates. I paused a moment to watch as they performed and knew that in their minds they were stars, basking in the approval of the strangers surrounding the plaza. Whatever dreams of celebrity or affection or approval those skaters had in their heads were surely being fulfilled, if only for the brief moments they spent on the ice below Prometheus' blank gaze. New York had always been a city for dreamers because it was a city that could make dreams come true. Which is why all those starry-eyed kids piled off trains at Grand Central or Penn Station or hopped off the buses at the Greyhound terminal on West Fifty-third Street and the All-American station just a short walk from the glittery promise of Times Square and Broadway, where dreams were a dime a dozen but where success was emblazoned in the lights of signs several stories high. There was the dream that David Reed had brought with him from Cleveland, the dream of being a star on a popular radio program that people listened to from coast to coast.

The line waiting to take the Radio City studios tour curled out of the NBC lobby into the long marbled corridors of the RCA Building, while a boy in a blue uniform dispensed the tour tickets from a glass booth at the foot of the plush red carpet that went up a wide stairway to the lounge where tours began. The boy gave me an impatient look as I stepped to the head of the line. "You'll have to wait your turn, sir."

"I'm looking for one of the tour guides. Robby Miller."

"Robby's not working today."

"Oh? Day off? Called in sick?"

"Just didn't show up for work is all I know."

"Is that unusual for him?"

The boy eyed the restless line of customers. "Sir,

there are people waiting." I gave him a look that told him I was not leaving until he answered my question. "Yes, very unusual."

"Do you know where he lives?"

"I do but we don't give out that information."

I pulled out my calling card and handed it to him. "Make an exception in my case, okay?"

"He lives in Greenwich Village."

"Do you know *where* in the Village?"

"The Broadway Central Hotel."

In its day, the hotel had been touted as America's most palatial, and it had been witness to some history. In 1876 the National Baseball League was organized in one of its rooms. Four years earlier in another, Edward S. Stokes shot and killed James Fisk, president of the Erie Railroad, in a quarrel over the actress Josie Mansfield. Across the street stood Wanamaker's department store and a block up Broadway where the world's most famous street had been forced to swerve because Hendrick Brevoort had refused to allow a favorite tree to be cut down to make way for the roadway stood the lacelike Grace Episcopal Church. The neighborhood had once been among the finest but had now become one of New York's shabbiest. The hotel clerk greeted me with as much warmth as the boy in the Radio City tour booth. "What are you, a cop?" he asked. When I showed him my card he shrugged. "A cop's a cop, even if he's a private shamus." He tossed my card back at me. "Robby Miller's not in." He looked at me through slit eyes with a what's-in-it-for-me-if-I-talk-to-you look. He was worth two dollars, no more, I figured, but what he had to say was no bargain. "He left the hotel last evening, around seven o'clock, climbed into a yellow cab and took off. Haven't seen him since."

"Maybe he came back while you were off duty."

The clerk nodded at the keys in a warren of mailboxes. "His room key's still there."

-86-

"But he didn't check out?"

"Skipped out is more likely."

"Why's that?"

"Behind in his rent."

"I'd like to see his room."

"That would be against the rules," he said, smiling a that'll-cost-you-at-least-five-bucks smile, "and probably illegal."

The fiver bought me the reasonable expectation that Robby Miller had not skipped out. People who skip out on their hotel bills take their possessions with them, and Robby Miller's possessions, such as they were, were in the room—a couple of shirts in the bureau drawers along with socks and underwear, a fairly new blue suit in the closet hanging next to his Radio City tour guide outfit, and a small envelope on the dresser containing a pair of balcony seats for the Ethel Merman musical for Saturday night. The goods meant Robby Miller planned to return to his room but gave no clue as to why he'd not shown up for work that day nor why he hadn't slept the night in his room.

Plenty of plausible explanations for Robby Miller's vanishing act presented themselves to me as I mulled it over on the uptown train, but as I walked east on Fifty-second Street toward my office above the Onyx, I entertained myself with a few of the little questions that Robby's absence raised. First, had Tinney and Brogan scooped up their star witness for safekeeping—perhaps to keep him from talking to me? If not, then did the cops know that Robby was among the missing, no matter how temporary his absence might prove? Had he simply been shacking up somewhere? Or had something else come up that was so urgently important that he risked losing his job at a time when his financial straits were narrow and perilous, to say the least?

As inviting as these questions were, they took a back seat when I got to my office and found stuck in the door a note written with the same extravagant style with which Rita DeLong played the organ. "I have turned up something very important concerning David Reed. Come to my apartment as soon as possible." Her address was imprinted at the top of the flowery stationery. It was just off Beekman Place where Fifty-second Street dead-ends above the East River, in the same building where Alexander Woollcott lived and which Dorothy Parker had bestowed with the name "Wit's End."

# 18

Rita DeLong was one of those women who must serve tea and cakes and show you through the apartment to point out the little treasures picked up in Venice and Paris and the Picasso print obtained in the south of France or in some little gallery on the Costa Brava before getting to the point. She was overdressed in a silk gown as flowery as her letter paper and the music on her daily radio program, but the parlor of her apartment was surprisingly austere in its furnishings, all chrome and glass tables with sharp corners and too-low chairs and couches with too-straight backs. The exceptions to this bleakly modern room were an elegant white grand piano in a bay window, a lovingly polished spinet organ of exquisitely mellow wood and dazzlingly spotless keyboards, and a wall of bookshelves filled with volumes on music and musicians and rows of record albums, single discs in tan paper sleeves, and dozens of sixteen-inch transcriptions. Of these on her tour of the apartment she proudly said,

"They are my programs from the last five years. Regrettably I don't have records of my work before that. I just never thought about it. It's only when you get older, Mr. MacNeil, that your past takes on aspects of treasure. Are you a man who keeps souvenirs?"

"I never did it in any organized way, but it's just as well because everything I had was lost in a fire five years ago. The trouble with mementos, Miss DeLong, is that they become a burden if you're not careful. You find yourself polishing and dusting all the time. Of course, my memories are not so pleasant. I was a cop all my life. If I'd saved mementos I'd have boxes full of mug shots and evidence. You happen to be one of those fortunate people who have a past that is filled with music."

"Somehow I sensed that you were a man with an appreciation of music. As for me, I've been in love with music all my life and I've been lucky to have had the privilege of bringing music to people through radio. I was one of the first women to have a radio program, you see, but there's a problem in having been a pioneer. People look at me as if I belong in a museum. The day comes when people you helped get their first jobs forget where they came from and who you are. I have never been that kind of person, thank the Lord. Perhaps if I'd been as hard as some others in radio I would have had a greater success, but at what cost? It's a pity that some people feel they have to trample on others, even after they've achieved success."

"Are you referring to Derek Worthington?"

She smiled coyly. "Of course. I'm not surprised that he met a violent end, but I know that sweet David Reed did not do it. With a phone call I can produce a witness to verify that David *was* watching the skaters at the time of the murder." Dumbfounded, I told her to make the call. She lifted an ornate French-style telephone, dialed, and said, "Come now, please." Gently placing the receiver in its cradle, she looked at me triumphantly.

"Would you care to know how I came across an eyewitness to David's whereabouts at the time of the murder?"

"I certainly would!"

"Well, it was all happenstance, you see. I attended a small dinner party last evening. It wasn't one of those typical Manhattan events that I generally decline invitations to. This was given by Woollcott, who lives just downstairs."

"Yes, I know."

"Have you been to *The Man Who Came to Dinner*, by the way? It's wonderful! It's based on Aleck."

"Yes, I know. About the witness?"

"Naturally the talk of the party was the dreadful murder of Derek Worthington, and of course, I was the main attraction. Aleck Woollcott fancies himself an expert on crime, especially murder, so he demanded all the details and I told him everything I knew. Well, when I was discussing the plight of poor darling David having no one to testify that he was outside at Rockefeller Plaza at the time of the murder, one of the guests spoke up and exclaimed, 'But he was. I saw him there!' Well, imagine my amazement. Immediately, I knew I had to contact you. I telephoned your office but you were not in. This morning I went there and you still were not in, so I left the note."

Impatiently, I asked, "Who was the guest?"

"His name is Enrico Avilla. He's a very talented vocalist. I've known him for several years. We are quite a small circle, those who are invited to Aleck Woollcott's affairs. Enrico and I have been discussing making records together, but I had not seen him since the murder. He was out of town for an engagement at a club in Philadelphia, I believe, but he had been in town on the night of the murder and was passing through Rockefeller Plaza. Enrico will tell you all of this in his own words when he arrives. He should be here very soon. Poor boy, he's been expecting my call all day."

"That was very good of him."

"Well, a young man's life is at stake, isn't it?"

"It surely is."

"When I think of what David and Maggie have been through it breaks my heart. I've been so fond of them. They are almost like my own children."

The half-hour it took for Enrico Avilla to arrive seemed more like several hours, but he came, a tall, swarthy Latin with slicked-back Vitalis hair and a figure as thin and straight up and down as a Flamenco dancer. He bowed slightly when we shook hands. He spoke with only a trace of an accent. He was obviously a trained singer, richly baritone and, I supposed, the kind of singer that his press agent would describe as seductive. He settled into a corner of Rita DeLong's uncomfortable couch and plunged into the story I hoped would spring David Reed from the Tombs and undo Tim Brogan's plans to send the kid to the electric chair.

"I had just left the home of a friend, where I had dropped in for cocktails, and was strolling toward my home when, on a whim, I cut through the Rockefeller Center Promenade to see the Christmas decorations. The tree is always so beautiful, the jewel of New York in the holiday period. I always enjoy watching the people skating in the rink and did so for a few minutes. When I turned to continue my walk I noticed Mr. Reed was also above the plaza watching the skaters. It was six-oh-five exactly." He paused and looked down at his gold wristwatch. "I was mindful of the time because I had an appointment at six-thirty."

"An appointment at home?"

"Why, uh, yes. I had invited a few friends for dinner."

"I see."

He fiddled with his wristwatch. "I looked at my watch. That's how I knew the time."

"You're sure it was David Reed?"

"Oh, yes. I've met David on several occasions. I'd recognize him easily."

"Well, it was rather chilly that evening and with David's overcoat collar turned up the way it was, you could have been mistaken."

"Oh, not at all. I got a good look at his face straight-on."

"Did he see you?"

"No."

"And you didn't speak to him?"

"I was in a hurry."

"Yes, it was a cold evening."

"Very."

"And you're willing to testify that even with his collar turned up you got a good look at David Reed's face and that because of your concern about not being late for your guests you were very mindful of the time."

"That's it exactly."

"You'll tell this to the police and to the district attorney?"

"I will."

"How long have you been living in the United States, Mr. Avilla?"

"I beg your pardon?"

"How long have you been living in the States?"

"Several years. I'm a naturalized citizen."

"Do you appreciate the penalties for perjury?"

"Perjury?"

"Really, Mr. MacNeil," exclaimed Rita DeLong. "What are you getting at?"

"I'm getting at perjury, Miss DeLong. That's what Mr. Avilla would be committing if he swore to this story in court." The organist and the vocalist exchanged sheepish defeated glances. "David wasn't wearing an overcoat that evening. If you're going to be a perjurer, Mr. Avilla, no matter how noble you may believe your motives to be and no matter how devoted you may be to Miss DeLong, first get your story straight. And what's more, your reason for looking at your watch is pretty feeble. You'd be torn to shreds on the witness stand."

Rita DeLong verged on tears. "We only wanted to help, Mr. MacNeil."

"Lies never helped anyone," I said as I got up and stalked toward the door. I stopped and looked back at the little woman who had made a grand but mad gesture in the name of friendship, seated primly in a chair with her delicate and talented hands knitting and unknitting nervously in her lap. "You are quite a package, Miss DeLong," I said, smiling.

"What you mean to say is that I'm a tough old dame."

Outside in the hard gusts of sleet off the East River below the windows of Wit's End I began to shiver at the thought of what Tim Brogan and Bill Tinney would have done if Rita and her Latin friend had gone to them with their invented alibi for David Reed instead of coming to me first. "God save us from the good intentions of our friends," I muttered into the wind as I flagged down a taxi.

It was turning into the kind of night when I felt sorry for cabbies and cops having to be out in the sleet and the wind. There are many grand, even excellent, things about New York City, but nights like this one weren't on the list. It was the type of night when sensible folks stayed at home parked snugly in front of their radios. My destination was the Biltmore Hotel. My aim was that I'd find in the taxi line at the Biltmore a kid named Davey Jericho. My hope was that Davey could come up with information concerning the whereabouts of young Robby Miller.

If you want to find out about anything, ask a New York taxi driver. Next to cops, cabbies know more about the life of the big city than anybody. When you spend twelve or more hours a day cruising the city streets and eavesdropping on what goes on in the back seat, you become an expert on the town and the people who make the town hum.

Nobody was better at keeping an eye on the big town than Davey Jericho.

## 19

If I needed Davey and he didn't happen to be waiting on the taxi line, I could always leave word for him with the Biltmore doorman. Davey made a point of working the Biltmore line because, he said, Biltmore guests were usually businessmen on expense accounts and therefore better tippers. Money was a big thing in Davey's life because he was studying law at night and hoping to turn a law degree into a job with J. Edgar Hoover's G-men.

Wanting to be a lawman had been as much a part of Davey Jericho as his wiry build and his good looks, which were more Italian than Jewish, for as long as I'd known him, which was all his life. His father had been my partner on the police force until he was killed in a gun battle with a two-bit mobster when Davey was only eight years old. In the fourteen years since, I had been the closest thing Davey had to a father, so it was my advice that he think about joining the FBI if being a lawman was all that important to him. "A G-man's got a lot better life than a cop," I explained, adding that to be a man on Hoover's team a guy had to have either a law degree or be an accountant. When the time came that he had a law degree, I planned to persuade Davey to forget carrying a gun and become a prosecutor instead, it being a fact that lawyers have a longer life expectancy than cops or G-men.

Davey was slouched in the front of his cab on the Forty-fourth Street side of the Biltmore. The moment he saw me he came up straight and grinning. "Harry, what's cooking?" The light in his eyes meant he had visions of being asked to shadow someone for me. The light dimmed a little when I told him that I needed to know who had picked up Robby Miller at the Broadway Central Hotel at seven o'clock last night and where the cabbie took him. "Sure, Harry. I'll ask around. It would help if I know what the guy looks like. Better if you've got a picture of him."

"The kid's one of the tour guides over at Radio City. You know the type. Clean-cut, boy-next-door looks."

"Ivy League looks?"

"Exactly."

Davey's face lit up brighter than before. "Say, is this connected to that Radio City murder?"

"You're too smart for me, Davey."

"I thought they made an arrest in that case?"

"They did."

"But the suspect didn't do it?"

I shrugged. "He says he didn't. His girl friend says he didn't."

"What do you say?"

"Too soon to say anything, Davey."

"Is she a number?"

"Who?"

"The dame in the case. The girl friend."

"She's sweet."

Davey shook his head. "You and my old man. Always a pushover for a sweet face!"

It was a short walk from the Biltmore to the Onyx.

Everything in Manhattan's a short walk. Only no walk anywhere is as short as the one from a death row cell at Sing Sing to the electric chair.

When I got back to the office, waiting in the front of one of the city's black Ford sedans to take me downtown to see a man whose job it was to start guys on that last short walk was Bill Tinney. "What the hell's the matter with Brogan?" I asked as I climbed into Tinney's car. "Hasn't he got anything better to do than waste my time?"

Tinney was laughing appreciatively as he headed toward Fifth Avenue.

## 20

With a face as Irish as his name and a build like a Notre Dame tackle, Tim Brogan had been one of the bright and brash young men on the racket-busting team of Thomas E. Dewey in the big push to toss mobsters like Luciano into prison. Brogan had begun his apprenticeship in law enforcement on the bottom of the ladder as a guard in the toughest reformatory in the country, the House of Refuge on Randall's Island. Days he spent shoulder to shoulder with the meanest punks in the city. Nights he spent hitting the law books. When the time came for Dewey to put together his little band of righteous storm troopers, Brogan was among the first chosen. Since then he had chalked up an impressive record as an investigator and prosecutor and come to head up the Homicide Bureau. When he scowled at me from behind his big desk in the D.A.'s office, I knew this was not going to be an amiable gabfest between a couple of old crime-war veterans. "What the fuck are you messing around the Worthington case for?"

"And a Merry Christmas to you, too, Tim," I replied cheerily.

Brogan was definitely not in a jolly mood. He made a gun out of his finger and thumb and pointed it at me. "You're way off base on this, Harry. We've got the Reed kid dead to rights and I don't want some private dick—not even Harry MacNeil—screwing it up. Who's brought you in on this case, some shyster Philadelphia lawyer or a commie bleeding heart from the Civil Liberties Union or what?"

"The kid's fiancée, as a matter of fact."

Brogan grunted and got up behind his desk. He stood with his back to me looking out a window that had an enviable view of the elegant Brooklyn Bridge. He turned, frowning. "The best thing you could do for this dame and her boyfriend is persuade the kid that it's all over and that he'll get a fair shake if he knocks off his hard-nosed insistence that somebody else blasted Derek Worthington. There isn't anybody else, and we can prove it."

"If you can prove it, then why all this crap about me talking Reed into signing a confession?"

"To save the taxpayers a lot of expense, for one thing."

"That's very civic-minded of you, Tim."

Brogan threw himself into his chair, still frowning. "You wouldn't be milking this Skeffington dame for a few extra bucks for your wallet so you can meet your Christmas bills?"

"Screw you, Mr. District Attorney." I turned to go.

"Hold it, Harry. I'm sorry. That was uncalled for. Sit down and let's talk. Have a drink. A little seasonal cheer?"

I sat, but I wasn't interested in his peace offering. "You're the second guy to suggest that I'd be doing David Reed a favor by persuading him to cop a plea. Tinney tried it. Now you. Do you know what that says to me, Timothy? It says that Tinney's given you a shaky case and you don't want to go into court with it."

"That's bull. I've sent guys to the chair with less than we've got on Reed." He counted off the points on his stubby fingers. "Add 'em up, Harry, and it spells conviction."

"Your arithmetic's as lousy as your grammar, Brogan. I can put all you've got into the tip of my pinky and you know it. You're scared your case will collapse. That's why you're trying to muscle me aside. Admit it. You make me laugh."

"The grand jury didn't laugh. Yeah. They've returned a true bill. The kid's indicted. Murder one. The hearing'll be tomorrow. I expect we'll go to trial in early January."

"You're really pushing this one, Tim. Why? Eyes on the next election?"

"I'll let that remark pass, Harry. Out of respect for our long friendship and previous professional relationship."

"All you've got is that Reed can't prove where he was at six-oh-five P.M. that night. Hell, I couldn't prove where I was at the time. Why not indict me?"

Brogan grinned and drummed his fingertips on his desk. "Don't tempt me, Harry."

"You can grin all you want, but you have as much of a case against Reed as you'd have if you'd'd've picked up the first guy you met out on the street and tried to nail him for the murder of Derek Worthington. Christ, half the city had it in for that guy. You might even say that the weasel deserved what he got."

"Harry, I'm shocked to hear a former decorated police officer utter such a thought."

"Everyone on that radio show had a motive."

"I know all about the reasons other people might have had for wanting Derek Worthington dead, but all the others can account for themselves at the time of the murder."

"What can you tell me about the deal that made Miles Flannagan show up one day with a piece of paper giving him sole ownership of *Detective Fitzroy's Casebook*?"

"You're whistling up the wrong tree, Harry. That's a valid document. We found Worthington's copy of it in his desk in his apartment up on Central Park West. Yes, we gave his place the once-over. I know when I have a good case, Harry, but I've been in this business too long not to cover my ass. I assure you that my boys have looked at every angle of this case. You can go around town chasing your tail if you want to, but you're going to come up with the same thing we came up with. David Reed did it. Do yourself a favor and dump this case. You don't need this kind of heartburn, Harry."

"I say Reed is innocent."

"Yeah, you always were one to be taken in by the story of some good-looking dame. You probably would believe in Santa Claus if some dame told you to."

"I do believe in Santa Claus," I said as I headed out of Brogan's office, "but not because some dame talked me into it. I happen to know there's a Santa. Why, at this very minute you can find him holding kids on his lap at Macy's Toyland."

# 21

"David's been indicted."

Maggie took the news gamely. "What happens now?"

"He'll have to go to court to hear the indictment read and to enter a plea. He'll spend the holidays in jail until the case comes to trial probably soon after New Year's. He's gonna need that lawyer, Maggie. The public defender he's got now would be demolished by the D.A."

"We can't afford the kind of lawyer you're talking about, Harry. Neither David nor I has much money."

"What about his family?"

"His father's a laborer in a Cleveland steel mill. He has no funds. He spent most of the last few years out of work."

"Maybe David's friends on the show could help out."

She shook her head. "They're not rich people. The only person who's fairly well-off is Rita."

"Yeah, well what about asking her?"

"I couldn't. She's got problems of her own. Rita's not a young person, Harry. She has retirement to think about. Oh, she's always talking about landing a big recording contract, but nobody's going to buy albums of organ music. Her music is passé. Today the people who buy records want big bands, swing. I don't have to tell you. Even worse, I'm sure that her radio program is going to be canceled. Please don't mention that to her. No, Rita is a good friend, but she can't help with this." Tears were hovering at the corners of her eyes. "You're all we have, Harry. You're the one who's either got to find the real killer or turn up someone who saw David at the plaza at the time of the murder."

I thought about Rita DeLong and her Latin singer

-100-

and their well-intentioned but pathetic attempt at providing the corroborating witness I needed. What Maggie was asking was impossible: Find someone who recognized David Reed's face among the hundreds around the Christmas tree, someone who for whatever reason also decided to check the time at that moment. If there was such an unlikely person, he or she had not come forward for any number of reasons, not the least of which was the thoroughly human desire not to get involved.

In spite of my bravado performances before Tinney and Brogan in scoffing at the case they had against David Reed, it amounted to a considerably persuasive argument for finding the kid guilty of murder. He wasn't the only one who had a reason to kill Derek Worthington, but he was singular in his inability to show that he didn't. Of course, in court he was not expected to prove his innocence. The prosecutors had the burden of proof of guilt, and on their side of the scales of justice were the fact that David Reed had twice exhibited a propensity for violence, once against Worthington himself, the fact that Reed had threatened Worthington, the fact that Worthington had denied Reed his big chance to be a radio network star, and the fact that Reed had no alibi when everyone else with a motive had an ironclad one.

I looked across the room at Maggie Skeffington's small-town-girl optimism. "Why the hell didn't your boyfriend get a sudden pang of hunger or something and buy a goddamned hot dog so someone would be able to step up and say, 'He couldn't've done it because he was chewing a frank with the works at the time!'"

Maggie fixed me with that Miss Molloy look of unbounded confidence. "You'll find a way to save him, Harry."

## 22

At Broadway, street-corner Santas and Salvation Army women in their blue-and-red uniforms, with tambourines in their hands, shivered beside money kettles and coaxed New Yorkers and tourists to dig into their pockets for coins to brighten the holidays of the hopeless. The dropping of a nickle or dime brought grateful "God bless yous." From a loudspeaker outside a record shop Bing Crosby was singing "Silent Night." A block away at Radio City Music Hall the line still ran halfway up Fiftieth Street. The movie was something called *Balalaika* with Nelson Eddy, Ilona Massey, Charles Ruggles, Frank Morgan, and George Tobias, but I doubted that anyone in that laughing crowd of holidayers was interested very much in an operetta about the Russian Revolution. They were on line for the Rockettes and the Christmas stage spectacular and the message of hope eternal written into the reenactment, complete with live camels and cows, of the birth of the baby Jesus.

Radio City Music Hall, like the big tree at Rockefeller Plaza, was a relatively new part of the city at Christmas time, but each had become as much a part of the city's Christmas as the smell of chestnuts being roasted by sidewalk peddlers, the displays of chic clothing in the windows at Sak's Fifth Avenue, and Toyland at Macy's. But on this cold and festive night just a couple of days before Christmas I couldn't share the joyful mood as long as David Reed was locked up in the Tombs for a murder I felt in my intuitive cop's bones he didn't commit though I was unable to prove it.

I walked east on Fiftieth to Rockefeller Plaza and stood for a moment on the corner opposite the great tree, then crossed over and bought a hot dog from the vendor who knew Maggie Skeffington by name. He slathered mustard on the hot dog and heaped it with sauerkraut. He handed me a frosty bottle of Coke. "On the house," he smiled. "Any friend of Maggie's is a friend of mine."

Astonished that he remembered me and afire with the possibility that this little hot dog man—Tony, I remembered, was his name—might have been selling his wieners at the moment David Reed was supposed to have been murdering Derek Worthington, I put the question to him.

Tony shook his head forlornly. "Nah. I don't remember seeing him, mister. I was here at the time. You work long days when you sell hot dogs, but if he was here at the same time I couldn't swear to it. There were thousands of folks in the plaza. I wish I could say I saw him. He's a nice boy." He shrugged and looked genuinely sad. Then another customer stopped at his cart and the business of hot dog selling resumed while I walked across the street toward the RCA Building.

In the middle of the long lobby at the entrance to the NBC studios a line had formed to buy tickets for the studio tours. The boy in the glass booth selling the tickets was not the one I'd talked to earlier, but he could have been his brother—the all-American-boy looks, the earnest gaze, the square jaw. He hadn't seen Robby Miller in a couple of days, he said, his cornflower blue eyes searching mine for some clue as to why anybody would be asking for a Radio City tour guide by name. "When's the next tour?" I asked.

"Leaves in five minutes."

I plunked down my forty cents and scaled the grand staircase to the mezzanine lounge, where the next tour waited for another of the boy-next-door guides to line them up and lead them into the mysteries of radio. We departed on the hour with a guide identifying himself as William Cole. "Welcome to Radio City," he began as he held open the doors of an elevator reserved for tours only. The elevator whisked us to the seventh floor and a small lobby festooned with publicity photos of those who were famous in radio. "Around us you see pictures of some of the stars of NBC programs," announced William Cole proudly. In his eyes glowed the expectation of finding his photo on these walls one day. I knew this because it was understood that the way to begin the climb to success in broadcasting was to get a job as a tour guide at Radio City. William had a voice that I could easily imagine coming out of a Stromberg Carlson radio.

William's audience of ten tourists and myself listened attentively as he pointed out the photos and named them in a seemingly off-the-cuff sketch of the history of NBC, starting with the tale of a young David Sarnoff, then a telegrapher for Western Union, picking up signals from the *Titanic* disaster in 1912, and then going on to form the Radio Corporation of America and the radio broadcasting empire in the midst of which William's audience listened to his speech with silent appreciation, even awe. "We'll now proceed to your left, down a corridor to one of the radio studios." He held out an arm to point the way and then hurried to the head of the group. As we passed the door to the control room for Studio 6B, William made no mention of the real-life drama that had been overheard at that spot. I looked at my wristwatch. The tour had begun in the mezzanine at three o'clock. It was now precisely 3:05.

"In this studio," said William as the group huddled around a vast plate-glass window, "we broadcast programs of news and information. You'll note that it does not have accommodations for a studio audience." It was a small gray room sparsely furnished—a gray table, several gray armchairs, and an assortment of microphones on the table and on floor stands. "Mr. H. V. Kaltenborn broadcasts from here," William noted. He waited a moment to permit the tourists to gaze admiringly at Kaltenborn's table, chair, and mike. Then he led us farther down the hall. "Perhaps you have been wondering," he asked as he walked, "how we go about creating the various sounds and background noises you hear on drama programs?" He stopped by a gray windowless door and smiled. "In this room I'll reveal to you some of the most highly guarded secrets."

With a mischievous grin and a flourish of his arm he pushed open the door to another studio, but unlike Kaltenborn's barren room this one was cluttered with the machinery, tools, gadgets, and implements of the sound-effects man. With obvious relish, he hopped onto a platform in the midst of the clutter. Immediately he plunged into the creation of moods and the setting of scenes— rain on a roof, an opening door, a man walking across a wooden floor, and a horse racing through gravel—an effect created with a couple of coconut shell halves and William's wildly galloping hands. His audience applauded and he took a little bow.

"Some effects can't be readily produced by a sound man in the studio," he continued, "so these are found on recordings." He stepped up to a truck like the one Jerry Nolan used on *Fitzroy's Casebook*, a boxlike affair topped by three record turntables and six pickup arms. He used one of the turntables and two pickup arms to show how a continuous sound of a motorcar could be effected simply by placing the second pickup arm on the record when the first had reached the end of the record. "We could drive this car nonstop to California if we had the time," he laughed. "You can imagine, I'm sure, that a sound-effects man is going to be as busy as a one-armed paper-hanger if it's an especially complicated program." The group chuckled and so did I, even though I'd heard Jerry Nolan crack the same joke. I assumed that Nolan had taught William a few of the tricks of his trade. "The purpose of sound effects is the creation of the illusion of reality," William said as he waved a hand at the array of equipment. "A good sound-effects man may employ all of this and the recordings at the same time if he is creative and plans his tasks well and makes effective use of time." Having made this claim he proved it by creating a scene in which a man leaves his house, crosses a wooden porch, descends wooden steps, crosses a gravel driveway, gets into his car, and drives away. "But suddenly it starts to rain," he announced. Immediately he created rain with rice on a sheet of tin. "The storm gets worse," he exclaimed. He shook a long sheet of metal to duplicate the sound of rumbling thunder. "The wind rises," he cried. With a turn of a knob on the sound truck he brought in wind from one turntable while another provided the noise of the automobile's engine. "On the other record," he pointed out, "there is a sound effect that we will need a little later, but because I'll be busy with other effects, you'll note that the record is already turning but with the volume control turned down." He shook the thunder effect again and kept the rain machine spinning. The wind and the auto engine roared on. "This fellow is in a hurry to get somewhere so he's willing to take chances," William was saying, "but ahead lies danger." He let go of the thunder effect for a split second and flipped up the volume knob of the third turntable. From the loudspeaker burst the lonely scream of a locomotive whistle. "Can it be? A train? A railroad crossing?" He paused as the wind, rain, thunder, car, and train whistle combined in the little studio to give the impression of impending disaster. "Oh, good Lord," he shouted. With a grin he turned and pushed over a cardboard box that spilled its contents of junk onto the floor with an earsplitting crash to rival anything that ever tumbled from Fibber McGee's hall closet. Instantly he shut down all the sound effects but those of the wind and the rain and left his audience with a numbing mental vision of carnage and desolation in the dark of a stormy night. The tour guide broke the spell by announcing that he would now show them a television studio. A woman asked him what television was and with a big grin the guide replied, "The future."

I hung back a bit as the tourists filed from the studio on their way to the future because I wanted to have another look at the layout of studio, control room, offices, and corridors so familiar to those who took part every week in *Detective Fitzroy's Casebook*. If David Reed was not Derek Worthington's murderer, then the killer had to be someone else connected with the show. Somewhere in the timing and the geography there had to be room for someone other than Reed to have gotten to Derek to put a bullet in his head and still be able to avoid suspicion. Assuming David Reed's innocence—and that was what I was being paid to assume—how had the real murderer managed to be in two places at the same time? How could Flannagan and the sponsor have been together at the time of the murder and yet one of them be a killer? How could the cast be within view of one another and one of them be the murderer? Or Guff Taylor be in the technicians' lounge and in Studio 6B at the same time? Jerry Nolan on the air and yet be a killer?

I had no answers when I caught up with my guided tour, sliding into the rear of the pack as the tourists waited for an elevator on the sixth floor to take them down to the starting point again. We were back in the mezzanine lounge exactly at four. The tour had taken one hour. In tours as in radio, apparently timing was of the essence.

"Does the time it takes to give one of these tours vary from one to another?" I asked the guide.

"Oh, no. We're very precise. At worst it would be only a minute or two. The tour lasts one hour."

"Were you working the night of the murder in 6B?"

The all-American face darkened with suspicion. "That was one of my nights off."

"Robby Miller worked that night, correct?"

"Yes."

"And Robby always ran his tours according to the schedule?"

"Certainly. Are you a police officer?"

"Private investigator."

"Well, believe me, there's no chance that Robby could have been wrong about the time when he heard that shot. Robby is precise about his work."

"I understand he didn't show up for work today, however."

"That's the first time that's ever happened."

"Do you know Robby well? Are you friends?"

"All of us guides are friends."

"Do you have any idea as to why Robby didn't come to work today without calling up or telling anyone in advance?"

"No, sir, I'm afraid not. It's very peculiar. His job is very important to him. He wants to get into radio and he knows that this is the way to start. Like me, he hopes to be an announcer. So I don't see why he wouldn't come to work. Yes, sir, it would have to be something awfully important for him not to show up."

"He didn't come home to his hotel room last night either."

William smiled mischievously. "He might have been with his girl friend."

"Ah, I hadn't considered that possibility. It's important that I talk to Robby. Do you happen to know where his girl friend lives?"

"Don't know that, but she works right here at Radio City. She's a secretary in the personnel department on the fourteenth floor. Name's Joan Byrne. Ask for Joanie. Cute little redhead."

## 23

Looking like a cop has its advantages, one of them being that people who assume you are a cop don't give you any arguments when you breeze into their office and ask to take one of their employees away from the job for a few minutes. The woman who ran the personnel department for the network was one of those people who go on instinct, and when her instincts led her to assume I was a policeman I let her believe it. The result was a chance to talk to Joan Byrne alone in a vacant office overlooking Rockefeller Plaza. She was a small girl with rusty-red hair and green eyes, a gal half the New York Police Department would have referred to as a colleen. She was not surprised to learn that Robby hadn't come to work that day. "It's not like him not to have phoned to tell them he wouldn't be in," she said. "Maybe he just forgot in the excitement of it all."

"What was Robby excited about?"

"He said he couldn't tell me everything right then, but that a wonderful opportunity had opened up for him. He called it a big break that would help him along in his career. Robby's not someone to make claims until he's sure of his facts. I assume he's working on lining up a new job or something like that. I hope so. He's very talented and deserves a break."

"He didn't come back to his hotel last night. Any idea where he spent the night?"

"None." She shook her head and frowned.

"Did you see him last night?"

"He called me up but I didn't see him."

"What did he say when he called?"

"Just that things were looking very good for him. For us. He was very excited. Very happy."

"But he didn't say why, only that he was onto something to help him in his career?"

"Is something wrong, Mr. MacNeil? Are you keeping something back from me?"

"Of course not. This is just routine stuff. Part of the investigation of the murder of Derek Worthington. A few loose ends."

"What a terrible thing that was. Poor Mr. Worthington. I feel sorry for that man they arrested, too. I wish Robby hadn't been the witness. I'll be glad when it's over with."

"Understandably, Miss Byrne."

"If I hear from Robby, should I . . . ?"

"Have him give me a call." I wrote down my phone number. "And don't worry. As I say, it's all routine."

I waited until I got back down to the lobby before calling the Broadway Central Hotel. The telephone operator tried Robby Miller's room and let it ring several times, but Robby Miller did not answer.

# 24

Swing Street in the daylight looked as useless and bleak as I felt, and my office with its Canal Street secondhand furniture didn't make me feel any more chipper. There was a pile of mail on the floor beneath the letter drop, but the leavings of the mailman were as unrewarding as everything else at that moment, a stack of bills and unwanted advertising brochures. Not even a Christmas card. I tossed the mail unopened on my desk, cocked back in my chair, pulled open the bottom drawer where I kept a bottle of Scotch and glasses, poured a tall one, and reached behind me to a shelf to flip on the radio. As if to underscore my lack of seasonal cheer, the set poured forth a helping of bubbly Christmas tunes played on an organ. It took me a moment to realize that I was listening to Rita DeLong's program. Maggie was right, I decided as I listened to Rita's "Jingle Bells." The day of the organ recital on radio was coming to an end. Tastes had changed, thanks in no small measure to jazz clubs like the one three floors below me. Jazz had led America into the swing era now being dominated by big orchestras playing music that kids wanted to dance to. Pretty soon the only place you'd be able to hear organ music was in church or at Radio City Music Hall. Radio listeners wanted big bands on the air direct from ballrooms or on records on shows like Martin Block's *Make Believe Ballroon* on WNEW.

Slouched behind my desk and sipping the warm Scotch, I figured that a good deal more than musical taste was going to change in the next few years. In spite of what isolationists and America Firsters like Charles Lindbergh and Father Coughlin espoused in their radio addresses, that the United States had no business getting involved in the European war, I knew—and I knew that FDR knew—that the United States would have to get into the fight eventually if Hitler, Mussolini, and the Japs weren't stopped in their tracks. All you had to do was listen to the news on the radio to appreciate that the Christmas of 1939 might turn out to be the last peacetime Christmas for Americans for a while. If we weren't in the war in 1940, I was certain we'd be in it in '41. Practically every night the radio gave us H. V. Kaltenborn, Quincey Howe, Gabriel Heatter, Raymond Swing, or Edward R. Murrow warning about the peril from the Axis, and if they weren't sounding the alarm, Churchill and Roosevelt were.

With civilization on the brink of possible annihilation, the plight of one kid with an Andy Hardy face and a murder indictment facing him probably didn't amount to much. Already other stories had pushed it off the front pages of the newspapers, while the Ben Turners of the town went chasing after new sensations. A case that had been the talk of New York a week ago now wasn't even news. There'd be a one-day splash when the indictment was announced, but then the case of *The People versus David Reed* would again be stuff for the editor's spike, at least until the trial was held. That event was a few weeks away, but every hour that passed made it less and less likely that Harry MacNeil, "the help of the hopeless," would be able to turn up anything to keep Reed from taking that lethal walk from death row to the chair.

I felt sorry for Maggie Skeffington.

And I felt sorry for myself.

I was still feeling that way hours later when Ben Turner knocked once and walked in, as was his custom. He stopped short in the doorway, his Adams hat cocked back, his hand on the knob. "Cripes, look at you." He slammed the door and sauntered to the desk, where he leaned on his knuckles, took a deep breath, and got ready to launch one of his what-the-hell's-eating-you inquisitions. "I haven't seen your jaw that low since you had money on the Giants in the '37 World Series." He came up straight, grinning, because he'd had the Yankees in that series, in which Joe DiMaggio had hit his first series home run and Lou Gehrig had hit his last. "Are you gonna mope in this crummy office all night or will you join me—I'm buying the drinks!—at the Cotton Club?"

Suddenly it dawned on me that Ben had the indictment of David Reed on his mind. "You heard, huh?"

Ben held out his arms in exasperation. "I get paid to hear. I'm a crime reporter for crissakes." He dropped his arms and leaned on his knuckles again. "What's an indictment, after all? Just an accusation. The People accuse." He lifted himself up again and pointed a stubby finger my way. "*J'accuse!* Well, plenty of guys have been indicted and walked out of court scot-free. Same thing'll happen to this Reed kid with you on the case. Anything new?"

"Don't know if it's new or even of any importance, but the kid who overheard the shot that killed Worthington didn't show up for work today and didn't sleep in his room last night."

Ben waved a hand. "Out getting his ashes hauled, prob'ly."

"His girl friend hasn't heard from him either."

"So he's got two girls. Maybe three."

I nodded. "Anyway, I've got Davey Jericho checking his cabbie friends to see if any of 'em picked up the kid at his hotel and where he went if anyone did."

"Harry, there's no way that kid could've done it. He was leading a gang of tourists at the time, remember."

"I took one of those tours today. Very interesting. You should do it sometime. They run like clockwork. If Robby Miller says he heard a shot at six-oh-five, then he heard a shot at six-oh-five."

"Was there ever any doubt about that?"

"There was hope, Benjamin. Hope." I pushed up from my chair and crossed the office to grab my hat and coat. "But there's not much I can do about any of this for now, so let's get the hell out of here. What we both need is a little hot jazz, huh?"

Ben was silent going down the steps to the street, but he was thinking, I knew, and I also knew that I wouldn't have to wait long to get the benefit of the Turner thoughts. In the blast of cold air on Fifty-second Street he took a deep breath, snorted steam, and said, "I know you probably don't want to hear this, Harry, but I'll say it again. Maybe you're wrong. Maybe, just maybe, Reed did kill Worthington. Maybe that feeling in your bones is wrong, Harry. I know your bones tell you Reed's innocent but—"

"That's what the bones tell me, Ben. You've got the same kind of bones. How many times have your newspaperman's bones ached to tell you that what you were hearing was the truth?"

"It's happened. There have also been times when my bones ached and they turned out to be wrong. What if yours are wrong? Maybe Brogan and Tinney are giving you solid advice. Maybe it's time to throw in the towel on this one. Can't win 'em all, you know."

"You're a big help, Ben. A big help. C'mon. Let's get drunk."

The Cotton Club at Broadway and Forty-eighth was a downtown incarnation of the famous joint that had thrived in Harlem in the days before jazz became downtown-respectable. The midtown spot was copied after the Cotton Club, which had held sway for a dozen years on 125th Street before it closed its doors on February 16, 1936, a victim of the Depression, unfortunate incidents of violence in Harlem, and a widening chasm between the Negroes who lived uptown and the downtown whites who looked upon their trips to Harlem as slumming. In time for the World's Fair, the new Cotton Club opened its doors at the point where Broadway and Seventh Avenue met in the heart of the Broadway theater district. Bill "Bo-Jangles" Robinson and Cab Calloway had headlined the opening of the Cotton Club show in the spring. In the summer Andy Kirk's orchestra held the fort, and now the headliners were Louis Armstrong and Maxine Sullivan. Ben Turner knew I'd been a sucker for Maxine Sullivan for years. If anybody could yank me out of my downbeat mood it would be Maxine Sullivan singing "Loch Lomond," "If I Had a Ribbon Bow," and "Tishomingo Blues."

It turned into a fine forgetful evening, but by the time the city had slipped into its predawn hum, Ben and

I were again at the Onyx for the jam session that usually closed the club. I took a turn on the clarinet, but it was not one of my better performances. When the band stepped down from the stand, Louie wiped up the last spill from the bar, and the lights came up to signal closing time, Ben muttered his good-nights and I plodded up the steps to face my barren office and the bleak realities of *The People versus David Reed*.

I was about to curl up on my couch to sleep when the phone rang.

"Harry? It's Veronica."

"Past your bedtime, darling."

"Yes, I know."

"Is that an invitation?"

"Come over and find out."

She was waiting for me in one of those long gowns from Sak's or Bergdorf's that classy women in classy apartments put on for the big seduction scene in classy movies, so I assumed that radio's best scriptwriter had dreamed up a scenario in which she was Jean Harlow and I was Robert Taylor. She drank martinis. I drank Scotch. "Detectives have always fascinated me," she said presently.

"Women have always fascinated me."

"A snappy retort straight out of a Sam Spade story."

"I happen to know Dashiell Hammett."

"I had a feeling you might."

"What gave you that feeling?"

"Oh, I know he was a detective once himself. I guess I just assumed that all detectives know one another."

"Do radio scriptwriters all know one another?"

"Derek used to say that there are only two hundred people in the radio business and we all know one another. I presumed it was the same with detectives. What's Hammett like?"

"He's a drunk."

"You say that as if being a drunk were a sin."

"In a way it is. Wasting anything is a sin and a person who's a drunk is wasting himself. I hoped that when Dash found success with his writing he'd stop wasting himself. He hasn't. I haven't seen him in a couple of years. Last time was three years ago. He helped me on a case, actually."

"How fascinating. Tell me about it."

"Oh, you don't want to hear old war stories."

"But I do."

"Why?"

"Let's just call it research. No, let's just say I find you fascinating."

"You do like that word."

"Who are you, Harry MacNeil? Who are you really?"

"I'm an ex-cop who's now a private investigator who'd prefer nothing better than to play clarinet with a top jazz band and leave the detective work to better guys than me."

"Oh, you're not so bad."

"Is that so?"

"I do know a little about you. You see, I had you checked out before Maggie came to see you. I didn't want her to make a mistake. When she said that you'd been recommended to her by a newspaperman, I made a couple of calls."

"A little of your own detective work? And what did you turn up?"

"That was the curious thing. I heard you were a straight guy but—"

"But what?"

"Well, you just said it yourself. You'd rather do something else than be a detective."

"Yet you told Maggie to go ahead and hire me?"

"Because I also learned that you were a guy who fought for what he believed in, especially if he believed that someone was about to take the rap for something you thought he didn't do. I found out that you like to take it easy, but you never do if you think someone is about to take it on the chin unjustly. You sounded like just the kind of guy who'd decide that David Reed is innocent and would do all he could to set him free."

"Thanks for the vote of confidence. Sorry if it's starting to look as if your faith were misplaced. Frankly, I've got nothing. You're right in that I do believe the kid's not guilty of murdering Derek Worthington. Proving it, however, is not going to be easy. If I can prove it at all."

"You're not going to give up?"

"Veronica, there comes a time when you have to face the facts. I fight for a cause, yes, but I'm smart enough to know when to recognize it when the cause is lost."

"You're just feeling low. I always feel low at three in the morning. There's something about this time of day that gets to you. F. Scott Fitzgerald once said that in the deepest, darkest part of the soul it is always three o'clock in the morning. Cheer up, Harry. The cause isn't lost. It's just three in the morning and you need a little boost."

## 26

Dawn was stirring the city into a roar when Veronica stirred next to me and woke up. I'd been awake smoking and watching her and thinking for almost an hour before she reached for me again. As I slid down next to her I realized that a lot of what I'd been thinking had been foolish nonsense and that as long as this beautiful woman and sweet and idealistic Maggie Skeffington thought enough of me to place their faith in me, I owed it to them not to chalk David Reed up as a lost cause quite yet. Besides, another day on the case might bring me the break I knew I would need if I were going to show Tinney and Brogan that they had the wrong guy locked up. That was all I'd been hired for, after all—to show that Reed couldn't have put a bullet through Derek Worthington's brain.

Later, when the sun was a little higher over the East River and Veronica was curled up warmly against me, I said of the late Derek Worthington, "For a guy with all his genius and successes he was a pitiful example of the human condition, wasn't he?"

Veronica stretched and sat up amid her satin pillows. "He had his dark side. But part of him was brilliantly luminous and it was easy to be dazzled by him."

"You had a yen for him even though he was a bully who tormented people. Nursing vendettas. Treating decent people like dirt."

"Sooner or later a woman who knew Derek fell in love with him. And out of love with him. You forgave him. You forgave him because he could be very good for a person's career."

"Rather than walk out on him, you stayed with him because he could help you in your career?"

"He *had* helped me. I hoped he would help me

again. He wouldn't if I betrayed him. We all make compromises, Harry. Don't tell me you haven't."

"Could it be that David Reed wasn't willing to compromise?"

"David didn't kill Derek."

"Everyone tells me that, but the cops believe otherwise."

"I'm a writer, Harry. I know people. I know that you've got to have the heart to be a killer. David Reed doesn't have it."

"If I'm going to prove that Reed didn't kill Derek, I'm going to have to give the cops the person who did."

"Let them worry about who did it. All you have to do is show that David couldn't've done it. That's all Maggie wants. That's all I want. Personally, I believe Derek got what he deserved, and if the real killer gets away with it, well, I wouldn't mind. I do mind that David is the one who's under arrest because I know he's innocent."

"This is not one of your scripts, Veronica. This isn't one of Dash Hammett's novels, either. This isn't a fictional murder with a trick ending on the last page that you cooked up on your Royal typewriter over at Radio City."

"And Harry MacNeil's not a fictional gumshoe on the radio. You're genuine, Harry. You're not an actor who's never been closer to a real gunshot than Jerry Nolan shooting off one of his sound-effects blanks."

Suddenly I sat bolt upright with a crazy idea. Then I grabbed Veronica and kissed her, and the next second I was out of bed and getting into my pants. "Honey, you are a genius."

Startled, she blurted, "Where are you going? What are you talking about?"

"I'm talking about the wonders of radio, gorgeous. Those magical illusions that come out of the loudspeaker night after night. I'm talking about a program that tricks its audience into believing it's coming from New York when it's actually originating in Chicago. I'm talking about rice on a sheet of tin and a door that opens to nowhere and fire made of cellophane. I'm talking about things that seem to be but aren't. I'm talking about a gunshot that somebody heard at six-oh-five P.M., only maybe they didn't hear a real gunshot at all."

# 27

Taking the steps two at a time up from the Onyx to my office, I found my head filled with vivid memories of images provoked by the wizardry of the sound-effects man—the clattering cascade of junk from Fibber McGee's closet, the wail of police sirens and the bursts of tommy guns on *Gangbusters*, the thunder of hoofbeats on *The Lone Ranger*, the preposterous coughs and wheezes of Jack Benny's Maxwell automobile, and the vivid sound portrait of William Cole's imaginary car careering to disaster with a speeding train. All figments of the imagination of the listener and the artistry of the sound-effects man. The thrilling enchantments of men like Jerry Nolan. Luckily—luck was becoming my friend at last—Jerry Nolan was in the office of the NBC Sound-Effects Department when I phoned to ask him to meet me. He sounded less than excited by the idea. "I'm on a pretty tight schedule today, Mr. MacNeil."

"You may be able to help me crack the Worthington case, Jerry." I thought I sounded like a character on *Fitzroy's Casebook*. "Can you meet me at Lindy's? I don't want us to be seen together at Radio City." The conspiratorial sound in my voice hooked him. He agreed to meet me at four o'clock.

One thing I'd learned about radio people was that they are always on time. They were slaves to the clock. So Jerry Nolan breezed into Lindy's at four sharp. We got a table in as quiet a corner as you could hope to get. "I need a crash course in recorded sound effects, Jerry." His face lit up. I was on his turf. When I told him about William Cole's expert performance as a sound-effects man, he beamed and boasted that he'd taught the kid everything he knew. "There was one thing he did that really interested me. When he was creating the illusion of a car speeding toward a head-on crash with an oncoming train—"

"A great bit of business, isn't it? Makes your skin crawl."

"One thing about it puzzled me."

"What's that?"

"How'd he know that at the moment he turned up the sound of the train whistle that the whistle would be there?"

Jerry was in the midst of demolishing a corned beef on rye by this time, but he put down the weighty sandwich and leaned over the table as if he were about to reveal a profound trade secret. "It's simple. The record was rolling dead-potted." He blinked at the puzzlement registering on my face. "When you have a record spinning with the volume knob cranked down, that's called dead-potting."

"Okay, but how was William so certain that when he cranked up the pot the train whistle would be there?"

"Because I planned it that way." The corned beef on rye was forgotten. The sound-effects man's eyes were alight. "That whole car-train crash sequence is precisely timed. It comes across as if it's totally improvised, but it isn't. I know because I teach those tour guide kids the routine. It takes hours of rehearsal before they get the timing down pat. At exactly two and a half minutes into that routine the train whistle is called for. The whistle is found at exactly one minute into the effects record. So it's just a matter of timing the script and noting on what word in the little narrative that the kid's reciting he has to turn up the pot and get the train whistle. It's called back-timing."

"I understand now, I think. What if I wanted someone to hear a sound, say, at five minutes after the hour?"

He reared back with a look of revelation in his eyes. "Say, you might be on to something, Mr. MacNeil."

"How would you go about creating the effect of a gunshot that you knew had to be overheard at exactly five after six?"

"I'd find a sound-effects record that I could start rolling, say, at six o'clock straight up and know that five minutes later the recording has a gunshot on it. Of course there's the problem of whatever was on the record ahead of the gunshot." He thumped a fist on the table, rattling the dishes. "But even that wouldn't be a problem if you made a special recording with only the gunshot on it!"

Grinning, I exclaimed, "I think that's what might have happened, Jerry."

He shook his head. "You've got other problems, though. Such as how you'd play the recording so that it would be heard in the hallway outside the control room. I know for a fact that it wasn't done on my equipment in the studio. All of my records of gunshots were stored in the locked bin beneath the sound truck."

"But we're talking here about a specially made record."

"Yeah, that's true, but even then it couldn't've been done on the sound truck."

"Why not?"

"Well, the truck was in the studio and so was Derek."

"Could the record have been played in the control room?"

"Guff Taylor was up there."

"Guff left the control room right after the dress rehearsal. There wasn't anyone in the control room after six o'clock."

"So you theorize that the killer snuck into the control room and put on the record, then left?"

"To establish an alibi for the moment the shot was to be heard by Robby Miller's tour group at six-oh-five."

"Christ, that's clever."

Excitedly, I said, "It could have happened that way."

Then Jerry was shaking his head. "Sorry. There's another flaw."

"What flaw?"

"Derek would have heard the sound effect. It would have come over the studio loudspeaker." He sat glumly for a moment, his eyes turned down at his half-eaten sandwich, his fingers drumming a tattoo on the tablecloth. Then the eyes came up alight with discovery. "Except—"

"Except what?"

"One of the studio mikes was left on. Am I right?"

"Yes. One of the studio mike switches was found to be on when Guff Taylor came back for the broadcast."

Jerry grinned. "Then Derek couldn't've heard the sound effect."

"Why couldn't he have heard it?"

"Because when a studio mike is on, it automatically cuts off the loudspeakers. It's arranged that way to prevent what we in the business call feedback. That's when you hear a loud squealing sound because the output of the mike is coming back into the mike from a loudspeaker."

"Feedback?"

"Feedback!"

"The automatic cutoff of the studio loudspeaker would have made it impossible for Derek to hear the gunshot on the recording that was rolling in the control room."

"Theoretically it's possible, but first you'd have to have someone who had the opportunity and the skills to make the recording of the gunshot and to set it up in the control room. You'd need someone with technical skills, Mr. MacNeil."

"Or you'd need someone who had learned enough of those skills to pull the scheme off."

"You're talking about some pretty sophisticated skills."

"Any more sophisticated than the ones you teach to the kids who conduct tours and put on that sound-effects demonstration?"

Chuckling and reaching for his sandwich, Jerry replied, "Nothing is more sophisticated than the art of sound effects, Mr. MacNeil."

"This is just a theory right now, Jerry, so I'd appreciate it if you'd keep this conversation under your hat. If it turns out to be more than theory, then I'm pretty sure the district attorney will want you to testify as an expert witness about things like dead-potting, feedback, and the subtle difference between a real gunshot and one that's recorded."

"That'd be an honor, believe me."

"If there's even a hint to anyone else in the cast that you and I have figured out how this murder might have been committed, the bird might fly the coop."

"Mum's the word." He scratched his chin. "It's a pretty wild theory, you know."

"It's the only thing I've got."

## 28

On any afternoon I could always reach Ben Turner by calling the Press Shack across from police headquarters. From the tone of my voice he knew I was cnto something that might spell "scoop" for his newspaper, so I had no problem in persuading him to meet me at the city morgue in the bowels of the red brick pile known as Bellevue Hospital. Of all Ben's assortment of sordid but helpful friends, none could be of more help in a murder case than Mike O'Reilly, a meaty Irishman who kept watch over the bodies that the city stored in the morgue until somebody came to claim the corpses or until the D.A.'s office and the medical examiner gave the green light for them to be hauled over to the Potter's Field on Hart Island. So far the body of Derek Worthington had not been let go for the elaborate services that his radio colleagues would undoubtedly hold for him at Campbell's Funeral Home, even though they all knew he had been a rat and a heel.

In addition to having a look at the remains of the man who had created and acted the starring role on *Detective Fitzroy's Casebook*, I wanted to have a glimpse at the official paper work that certified that Derek Worthington had been a victim of a homicide and the precise manner in which his demise was achieved.

The route to the morgue was through a maze of hallways and down a flight of steel stairs, then along a dim and chilly passageway to a pair of black windowless doors. Beyond them was a cavernous room lined with polished steel refrigerator doors, iceboxes for those for whom the city of dreams had been the end of the road, most of them having come to that end through violence. Mike O'Reilly was seated at a desk just inside the room. He was dressed in the white uniform of his trade. A white surgical mask hung below his double chin. "Oh, Christ," he grunted as he pushed himself to his feet, "here come the Bobbsey Twins of crime." The brogue was second-generation Brooklyn-Irish.

"The Worthington case," announced Ben without preliminaries. He and O'Reilly did a lot of business together and amenities had long since gone by the boards.

O'Reilly sauntered down the room to the drawer where Derek the rat was waiting for someone to come and collect him. The slab rolled out at O'Reilly's deft touch and the sheet covering the body was drawn back to the shoulders. "One .38-caliber slug at the back of the head just above the neck. You want the medical terminology?"

"I'm just a dumb old ex-flatfoot, O'Reilly. Skip the big words."

"He was either seated or bending over when he was shot. The bullet coursed upward and to the left and exited above the ear. You can see where the ear used to be." There wasn't much remaining of the left side of Worthington's head but the face was reasonably intact. He'd been a handsome man but, of course, he didn't look at all the way he had sounded to me on the radio. "Death was instantaneous. Never knew what hit him," said O'Reilly matter-of-factly. "Want to have a closer look or shall I put him back?"

"Put him back."

The drawer slid into its place with a quiet but solid finality. "Now you probably want to see the reports?" asked O'Reilly, walking back toward his desk.

"Just the part about the time of death," I said, following.

O'Reilly shrugged. "I thought that was precisely known from other evidence."

"Yeah, but what did the M.E. list it as?"

O'Reilly searched the files in the bottom drawer of the desk and came up with the Worthington folder. He flipped it open and turned a few pages. "Anywhere between six P.M. and seven P.M., it says here." He handed me the folder.

In the precise handwriting of the medical examiner I found the notation of the more imprecise time of death as determined by medical science and the notation of testimony at the scene of the murder that a shot had been heard at exactly 6:05 P.M. by Robby Miller and his tourists. "Thanks, O'Reilly," I said, handing back the file. "You've been a big help."

Outside in the naturally cold air of First Avenue, Ben Turner grumbled, "So what did that prove?"

"Only that Worthington was killed sometime between six and seven o'clock."

"We knew that already."

"Yes, but what if Robby Miller's tourists didn't hear a gunshot at six-oh-five?"

"Harry, there were fifteen of 'em and they all heard it."

"They heard what they thought was a shot."

"It was the sound of a gun going off, Harry."

"Exactly! The *sound* of a gun going off. A sound effect. Think of the implications if they heard a sound effect and not a real shot. If that's what happened, then Derek wasn't killed at six-oh-five, he was shot later, and if he was shot later, then David Reed may not be the only one without an alibi. We know where everyone was at six-oh-five, but we don't know anything about their whereabouts later, when Derek Worthington may actually have been murdered."

## 29

I didn't have to be Dr. I.Q. to know that the only way to prove my theory was to find the recording with that gunshot on it, but the chances of finding it, if it existed, seemed as good as the odds on finding the proverbial needle in the haystack. The RCA Building provided an ample supply of nooks and crannies for stashing almost anything. There must have been, I figured, thousands of recordings stored in hundreds of slots in half a dozen studios and even more offices. And even if I found a recording with nothing else on it but one gunshot, it wouldn't guarantee a conviction in a court of law even if I managed to connect that recording with a plausible suspect in the murder of Derek Worthington. The only thing my theory gave me to go on was the possibility that Worthington was not killed at the exact moment when Robby Miller was leading his goggle-eyed tourists past that open control room door but later. Later, a lot of people might not have alibis at the ready, and because the main point against Reed was his lack of an alibi, I might at least be able to persuade Brogan that his case against Reed was worthless and, thus, spring the kid. In the end that might be all I would ever achieve in the case of the Radio City murder, but keeping an innocent man from going to the chair would be a pretty good day's work in anybody's book.

Back in the office, I picked up the telephone and called the Broadway Central Hotel. As far as anybody there knew, Robby Miller had not returned since he hailed a cab and headed off for parts as yet unknown. There was no word of any kind from Davey Jericho, so I assumed that my hackie friend was still working on the assignment I'd given him. There were plenty of cabbies in Manhattan and locating the one who picked up Robby

Miller outside his hotel would take time. If that cabbie could be located at all.

That sudden vanishing act bothered me. While it was certainly possible that the kid had a very ordinary reason for taking off, a little warning signal kept going off in my head. In one of Ben Turner's favorite phrases, "It wasn't kosher." Young Robby Miller had come across as a fellow who wanted to make a career for himself in radio. Landing a job as a tour guide or pageboy at Radio City was a leg up toward that career. Not showing up for work without giving notice would be a black mark on his record. I also didn't care much for the fact that Robby Miller's girl friend didn't know where he was. Not at all kosher. One thing I was sure of was that Robby Miller didn't kill Derek Worthington. The tour he'd been leading took an hour to complete, so Robby Miller's whereabouts could be vouched for by the tourists in that group he was leading at the time of the murder. So if guilt wasn't the reason for the kid dropping out of sight, what was the reason?

I still had no answer to that puzzler when I walked over to Radio City in the afternoon to attend the rehearsal for the next episode of *Fitzroy's Casebook*.

"All right, cast, let's get down to business." It was Miles Flannagan calling the actors of *Fitzroy's Casebook* to rehearse, and while I understood that he had no choice but to go on as before, I couldn't help feeling uneasy about the show going on as usual. The made-up story of *Detective Fitzroy's Casebook* seemed like meaningless stuff considering all that had happened and considering the fact—I had no doubt about it—that one of the cast was the real killer.

The second rehearsal for "The Case of the Black Widow," which was to be the Sunday-night offering on *Detective Fitzroy's Casebook*, appeared to me to proceed flawlessly, but it turned out that the time of the program was off by three minutes. Concerning this problem, Miles

Flannagan cheerily announced that the script would be cut to the proper length in time for the dress rehearsal the next day at three, after which the program would be transcribed for broadcast Sunday evening. "For the first time in living memory," Miles continued with a laugh, "we are all going to have a Sunday off. And every Sunday after that thanks to the miracle of electrical transcription. And long overdue, I might add, intending no respect for the not-so-dear departed."

Maggie was surprisingly unforgiving of the remark as we rode down in the elevator with Rita DeLong, Ben Loman, Sheila Fay, and Bart Mason, most of the cast of "The Case of the Black Widow," while Jason Patrick, Veronica Blake, and Miles Flannagan retreated to Miles's office to work on the too-lengthy script. "Miles didn't have to make that crack about Derek," she said. "It just wasn't right!" She shuddered a little. "It's as if Miles is dancing on Derek's grave."

"Pretty hard to do considering they haven't buried Derek yet," cracked Bart Mason. He made a face and threw up his arms defensively. "Sorry, Maggie."

"Miles has rushed in pretty fast," suggested Ben Loman.

"Someone had to," Maggie exclaimed, suddenly Miles's defender.

"Yes, of course," replied Loman, retreating, as was everyone else, before her wrath.

The streets around Radio City were doing their best to contribute to the roar of the town as we came out of the RCA Building on the Fiftieth Street side. The line at the music hall was as thick and long as ever despite the bitterly cold wind whipping eastward from the Hudson River and a cold crimson sunset. Maggie and I faced into the wind toward her hotel. The others raced to hail taxis, but Rita planted herself at the crosstown bus stop for the cheaper ride that would take her within a block of her place at Wit's End. She blew Maggie a kiss as we parted.

"That old dame cares a good deal for you," I said to Maggie as we trudged toward the Bristol.

Maggie punched my arm. "Don't call Rita an old dame."

"Well, she is."

"Aging but not old. You can be damned heartless at times, did you know that? You men don't understand about aging. You all do it so gracefully. The years add character to a man's face. It's not so for women."

"Is that why Derek dumped Rita? He just got tired of the older woman?"

"Harry, I'm not a gossip."

"Well, I am."

She punched me again and laughed. "There's a young man she's taken a fancy to and she's worried about the proprieties of what I will politely refer to as a December-May romance."

"Her passion for Derek was definitely a thing of the past?"

"You do know all the gossip, Harry! Yes, it was over. If something like that can ever be truly finished. Enrico has been good for Rita."

"Love affairs on the rebound can be risky business. That's especially true when she's December and he's May. Rita's a good friend of yours, so I hope you'll keep in mind the real possibility that this Enrico guy may be out to take her for all she has."

"What a cynic you are, Harry."

"Well, I've seen the results of quite a few December-May romances on slabs in the morgue."

"I assure you that Enrico is devoted to Rita."

Devoted for sure, I thought, if he was willing to risk perjury at her request. "You're pretty devoted to Rita yourself. Were you by chance using her shoulder to cry on that night in the cafeteria after your row with David?"

"It wasn't a row. Just a spat. It all seems stupid in hindsight. If David and I hadn't argued he would have been in the cafeteria with the rest of us."

"You're *positive* everyone from the cast was there?"

"Yes. We all got there around the same time. Taking into account stops at the powder room. At five after six we were in the cafeteria. I looked at the clock. Radio people are always looking at the clock."

"So I've noticed."

"We were all having a good time. Relaxing between shows. That's an especially nice time in the cafeteria. There are a couple of shows on the air from Radio City on Sunday evenings. It's quite a party atmostphere when we all get together in the cafeteria. We were all there, however. The whole cast of *Fitzroy's Casebook*."

"Except David Reed wasn't there."

Maggie's eyes filled with tears, but she held them back. "No."

"Guff Taylor wasn't there. He was in the technicians' lounge playing cards until a few minutes before seven."

"Yes."

"Miles was in his office having a conference with Mr. Richards until almost air time."

"That's true."

"What time was it when all of you from the cafeteria returned to the studio?"

"A few minutes before seven."

"The cast, the technician, Miles, and Mr. Richards all came back to the studio at about the same time?"

"Yes. Jerry Nolan came in at almost seven exactly. He always got back at the last minute because he was on the air on another show."

"And Reed came back just before air time?"

"Yes. Harry, what's this all about? What does it matter when we returned to the studio?"

"What matters is that everyone can account for his or her whereabouts and David Reed can't."

"I still don't see . . ."

I told her my theory and she became understandably

excited by it, but that vanished when I told her that the theory didn't count for anything in the face of the fact that all the other possible suspects had ironclad alibis. "Each of you can prove where you were the whole time between the end of the dress rehearsal and a couple of minutes before air time. All of you but David Reed. So even if Derek weren't shot at five after six but a little later than that, and even if I could prove it, it would still leave only one of you unaccounted for. And the only one in that unhappy category is your boyfriend."

She shook her head angrily. "No. That is not possible. Someone not connected with the show must have done it."

"Maggie, people do not walk into Radio City and into a studio without being seen."

"I will not believe that David is a murderer."

"Look at the facts, Maggie. Everyone connected with the show has an ironclad alibi. The whole cast was with you at the time. Guff Taylor is accounted for. Miles Flannagan and Mr. Richards were together. Jerry Nolan was working on another show. David's the only one left."

"But your theory about a fake gunshot—"

"A theory. One that makes sense only if I could prove that Derek was killed later and that it would have been possible for someone else to have gone into the studio and killed Derek at that later time. That theory doesn't wash anymore, Maggie. I'm sorry, kid, but all the evidence points to the police being right. I think he did it. I know that hurts you and that I've disappointed you, but I have to deal with the facts, the evidence."

"If that recording exists it would prove David's innocence?"

"It would knock a pretty big hole in the case the D.A. has built up."

"I'll find that recording, Harry. If it exists—and I'm sure it does—I'll find it."

"Maggie, leave this to me, okay?"

She shot to her feet. "I'm going to turn NBC upside down to find that record."

She was gone before I could say anything more, turning and hurrying toward the studios, leaving me staring after her in amazement at all that love Maggie Skeffington had for David Reed and all that Miss Molloy doggedness.

# 30

The next day was the day before Christmas. I awoke around eight with a hangover, a taste in my mouth like an old sock, and the unhappy thought in my head of the lousy present I'd given to Maggie for Christmas. If I'd had the chance to ask Santa Claus for a gift at that moment, it would have been one tiny little crack in the solid wall of evidence that surrounded David Reed as surely as the walls of the Tombs, but no matter how hard I looked at the case from all angles as I sat at my desk and drank warm Scotch that morning, I came up with nothing except my preposterous idea that the shot Robby Miller heard had been a sound effect and that the real shot that killed Derek Worthington had been fired later. The theory held up only if I could show that someone else from *Detective Fitzroy's Casebook* had had an opportunity to settle a score with radio's most famous fictional detective, but they all had alibis as neatly wrapped and tied with ribbon as any gift from Macy's. Try as I did to find a crack in the case, I only found myself running low on Scotch, lower on morale, and facing a coal-in-my-stocking Christmas when the phone rang and over the line chirped the jingle-bell cheeriness of Rita DeLong's voice. "You are a genius, Harry MacNeil, an absolute genius. What wonderful news from Maggie this morning. She called to tell me of the marvelous breakthrough you've had in the case."

"There's been no breakthrough, Rita."

"I refer to the recording of the fake gunshot."

"There was no fake gunshot, there is no recording."

"But of course there is," she laughed. "There has to be. Maggie and I are going to find it for you."

"Rita, come to your senses."

"Maggie and I are going to search Radio City from top to bottom until we find that recording."

Before I could say another word she hung up, laughing as she did so, like a little girl dismissing with ridicule and scorn the cruelly smug assertion from an older kid that there is no Santa Claus. I made no effort to get Rita on the phone again nor to telephone Maggie to talk them out of their search for a recording that I knew did not exist. I figured the only thing I could do was let them go ahead and find out for themselves that my theory was just a cockeyed pipe dream.

My bottle of Scotch was running on empty when the phone rang again at nine o'clock. It was Ben Turner and his voice was not ringing with holiday cheer. "Stay put, Harry. I'm picking you up in five minutes."

He sounded like a reporter who'd been up all night chasing the story that would get him a Pulitzer Prize. "What's cooking, Ben?"

"That kid who gave the tour at NBC the night Worthington was killed?"

"What about him?"

"They just found him dead in the East River."

## 31

I could smell the place a couple of blocks before we got there, a dismal sprawl of territory that was the backyard for fashionable Murray Hill, where slaughterhouses, breweries, laundries, and power plants spiced the air with bad odors and a mist of soot that was so pervasive that when it snowed the snow came down black. The area was still called Kip's Bay even though the bay had vanished years ago along with the pretty colonial farms that had rolled along the East River when Jacobus Kip owned 150 acres, Marie de la Montagne reigned in a grand mansion, the De Voors farmed, and Mrs. Murray was said to have detained a British general while George Washington's army escaped after the Battle of Long Island. The elegant town houses of the nineteenth century had given way to eyesore slums and nasty neighborhoods of the East Thirties, where in the murk and slime of the water just south of the tip of Belmont Island an East Side kid had spotted the bobbing corpse of young and ambitious Robby Miller, a bullet hole in the middle of his back. When Ben and I arrived, guys in overcoats over white suits were grappling him out of the river so that they could haul him to Bellevue and the morgue, just another piece of dead meat on a slab, as if he were a carcass from one of the meat-packing houses nearby.

I was not surprised to find Bill Tinney at the scene. He was not surprised to see me turn up. "I figured this little Hebe reporter would give you a call," Tinney said, sliding his gray fedora back from his forehead. He flitted a smile in Ben's direction. "The little cocker's got more connections than the Pennsylvania Railroad." He glanced down to the spot where the men were struggling to haul the body up a pile of icy paving stones dumped there who knew how many years ago. "Whoever did this thought they'd stripped the kid of all his identifying papers, but jammed down in an inside coat pocket we found a letter to him from his mother. It's Robby Miller, all right. Drilled smack in the middle of the back apparently. The slug probably made instant mincemeat of his heart. I'd guess he never knew what killed him. Or who."

"Ah, bullshit, Bill. He knew who killed him."

Tinney shook his head. "You're not going to try to connect this to the Worthington murder?"

"The hell I'm not. It's as plain as the dimple in your chin for crissakes, Bill."

"Harry, you sure do make amazing leaps of the imagination."

"I can see the wheels turning in your addled brain already, Bill. Putting this down as some cheap stickup or something equally absurd."

"Absurd is it? In this neighborhood?"

"He wasn't killed in this neighborhood and you know it. He was just dumped here. Where's there a better place to dump a corpse? Huh? How many uptown killings wind up in these waters, Bill? You've been a cop too long to believe that this kid was murdered around here. You'd like it to be that way, though."

"What's it to me where he was killed?"

"I'll tell you what it is to you. It's a hole a mile wide in your case against David Reed."

Tinney laughed, but it was that nervous kind of laugh you hear from a guy who's cornered and knows it. "Bushwa. Nothing but a coincidence."

"Coincidence?" Now Ben Turner was laughing.

"There's a connection between the Worthington murder and this one, Bill. You know it and I know it. And one of us is going to prove it whether the other one likes it or not," I said, striding away.

Ben had to scamper to catch up with me. "Now what, Harry?"

"The Miller kid took off from his hotel the other night in a hurry. Hailed a taxi to get to where he was going. I hope Davey Jericho has the answer to where the kid was headed. Find out who Miller was going to meet and maybe we find out who killed him and why, although I have a pretty good notion as to why."

Ben was puffing hard from hurrying as we climbed into his car. "Are you going to tell me or shall I wait and read all about it in the newspapers?"

"Can't you smell it, Ben?" I sniffed the rancid air. "The unmistakable aroma of blackmail."

# 32

Davey Jericho's hack wasn't in the line on the Forty-fourth Street side of the Biltmore Hotel, but I knew he'd show up there sooner or later because Davey always worked his way back to the Biltmore line no matter where his fares took him. He would even pass up fares trying to hail him on the street if he was close to his usual haunt just to get back to the high tippers at the hotel. There were half a dozen hacks on line when Ben Turner parked his car.

I knew all the drivers, either from my friendship with Davey or my days on the police force, a few of which I'd spent in the bureau that handled complaints against the cabbies, all of whom had had a hard time of it in the cutthroat days of hacking it in New York City. They all knew I'd come looking for Davey Jericho and I supposed they all knew why, but it was an old-timer, Sid

Ruderman, who sauntered in my direction as I eased out of Ben's car.

I knew Sid from the days when the gangsters were muscling in on the hack business by strikebreaking for the owners or by trying to take over the union—whichever side promised the better payoff for the hoods. In those days Sid lived uptown on the West Side with his new wife, Rosie, who cooked the world's best potato latkes and gave parties at which latkes were the main course and the entertainment afterward was some dizzy parlor game she remembered from her schoolgirl days or summer camp. Sid had started out with the Mogul Checker Manufacturing Company, which had come into the city with a fleet of hacks designated by a checker stripe and took away almost all the business from the Yellow Cab Company, which had taken it away from the Twentieth-Century Brown & White Taxicab Owners Association. Sid was driving Yellows when the first big strike was called and he nearly died in one of the battles that erupted on taxi lines all over town at the time. Sid also took Davey Jericho under his wing after Davey's father was killed. Sid had a shambling walk, an Old Testament face, and a droll sense of humor, the kind that hits you with delayed action, but he was all business this time. "Davey said if you should come around to tell you that he's at the coffee shop in Grand Central." It was obvious Sid knew what Davey was working on for me, but he also knew that it was for Davey to tell me what he'd learned, if anything, so he let it go at that.

I told Ben Turner he didn't have to hang around if he wanted to go home and get some sleep, but Ben's generous nose was sniffing the sweet smell of a big story, so he hiked around the corner with me to Grand Central. Davey was slurping soup at the counter of his favorite greasy spoon on the lower level. "Soup," I said as I sat on the stool next to him, "is not a musical instrument."

"Harry! Ben!" Davey grinned over his spoon. He was

careful not to slurp. "The case must be getting hot with the two of you shlepping around on Christmas Eve." I told him about Robby Miller being dragged from the East River. Davey put down the spoon, frowning. "Damn. I'm sorry I didn't come up with anything for you about the taxi he took from that hotel of his, Harry, but I only just learned this morning that it might have been one from the Hudson Cab garage over on Tenth Avenue and Forty-third. I just haven't had a chance to follow up." He stared down at his steaming vegetable soup. "If I'd gotten this lead sooner, maybe the kid wouldn't've . . ."

"Nah. I'm pretty sure he was killed the same day he left his hotel. He'd been in the water a day, at least, maybe a day and a half. Maybe two days. Plus, there's no guarantee that finding out where he took that taxi to will be of any help."

"Are you going to check it out anyway?"

"Sure. Maybe I'll get lucky."

"Want me to drive you over to Tenth and Forty-third?"

"Ben's got his car and Ben is not about to let me shake him off. You finish your soup symphony. I'll let you know if your legwork turns up anything."

"No trouble for me to come along, Harry," he said, smiling hopefully.

I slapped down a dime for his soup and coffee and a five-dollar bill. "Buy your girl friend something nice for Christmas."

Davey made a sour face. "We broke up."

"Then spend the five on your mother. And tell her I'll be around to wish her a happy New Year."

"You know, Harry," said Ben as we came out of Grand Central onto Vanderbilt Avenue, "maybe you ought to marry Mrs. Jericho. She's a good woman."

"Yeah," I said, pulling open the door of Ben's car, "too damned good for me."

## 33

There were three kinds of people in Hell's Kitchen—those who worked to get out and into successful and respectable lives, those who got out by getting into the rackets, and those who couldn't get out and would spend their whole lives on the mean streets and in the depressing tenements west of Times Square between Penn Station on the south and Madison Square Garden on the north and the Hudson at their backs. No stretch of turf in the world had coughed up so much trouble as Hell's Kitchen. In its heyday Hell's Kitchen gave New York the likes of the Hudson Dusters and the Gophers and such charming personalities as Newburg Gallagher, Marty Brennan, Stumpy Malarkey, Goo Goo Knox, and Mallet Murphy, whose hallmark was clubbing his victims with a mallet. These hooligans had held sway in dives and hovels on blocks known as Battle Row, Cockroach Row, Mulligan Alley, and in one especially sinister dwelling on West Fortieth called the House of Blazes. Ben Turner knew the area well and had turned out a series of articles in his newspaper on the colorful history of the territory, which, happily, had been cut into lately with the construction of the Lincoln Tunnel. On the plus side of that sordid history was the saga of the Fighting 69th, the Rainbow Division, which had covered itself with glory in the Great War under the leadership of Wild Bill Donovan and the spiritual guidance of Father Duffy, who forged the Hell's Kitchen toughs into a regiment that could come home from the war and march up Fifth Avenue to the cheers of a grateful city.

On this Christmas Eve twenty-one years after the war, Hell's Kitchen was as docile as Park Avenue when Ben turned from Forty-second Street onto Tenth Avenue and pointed the car toward the garage of the Hudson

Cab Company. The curbs were lined with yellow hacks, it being a Sunday and the day before Christmas and the taxi busines at low ebb. Ben double-parked and we went inside to find the dispatcher, a squat guy with a huge beer belly and a stogie stuck in the corner of his mouth. His name was Murphy and he'd been around long enough to know that we weren't looking to charter one of his hacks for a trip out of town. "Are you guys cops?" I showed him my identification. "A private dick. I can always spot the heat. Whatcha want to know?"

"Who was working the line at the Broadway Central the other night and where a certain guest at the hotel went," I replied as Murphy reached for a stack of trip sheets. I gave him the date and approximate time and he shuffled through the reports. He pulled out a sheet and handed it to me. The name of the driver was Thomas Damato. He'd had a busy night. The entries on his trip sheet ran down both sides of the paper. I found the entry I was looking for and handed the sheet back to Murphy. "Is Damato around today?"

"Off for the holiday. Tommy's very religious. Always takes off Christmas Eve and Christmas. Lives in Far Rockaway."

"That's a long haul into work every day."

Murphy yanked the cigar from his mouth and shrugged his beefy shoulders. "These days a guy gets work where he can, ya know?"

I thanked Murphy but didn't say anything to Ben until we were outside. He asked if we were now going to head out to the Rockaways. I shook my head. "Nah. No need to. There's nothing Tommy Damato can tell me that his trip sheet didn't tell me."

"Which was what?"

"Who killed Robby Miller and Derek Worthington."

Ben gaped at me for a moment and when I didn't say anything more blinked and blurted, "Are you gonna enlighten me or not?"

"Not right now, Ben."

"Why in hell not?"

"Because I have no proof."

"How do you get the proof?"

"You answer that question, Ben, and Mr. Anthony will award you seventy-five silver dollars." He looked glummer than I felt, so I gave him a cheering smile and slapped him on the back. "Buck up, old pal, we've been in worse spots than this, so get this crate started and drop me off at my office."

"What are you up to?"

"I'm going to try my hand at writing a radio drama."

"You're going to do what?"

"I'm going to write a script and have the cast of *Detective Fitzroy's Casebook* act it out for me. Complete with music on the organ by Rita DeLong and sound effects by Jerry Nolan."

"What the hell do you know about writing a radio script?"

"Very little, Benjamin, but I have one of Veronica Blake's scripts to use as a model, so how hard can it be?"

"And what do you expect to accomplish with this piece of creative writing?"

"Why, I'm going to do the same thing Hamlet did. What was it he said? Something about the play's the thing to catch a murderer?"

## 34

I wasn't at my desk more than five minutes before the phone rang and Maggie Skeffington started talking a mile a minute. "We've found it, Harry. We've found it. Just as you said. We've got that recording. Oh, Harry, come right away. Come and see what we've found. Come over to the studios right away."

The bells of Saint Patrick's Cathedral were chiming for the noon mass as I crossed Fiftieth Street and made for the entrance to the NBC studios. There was the usual line of tourists buying tickets for the privilege of peering into the secrets of radio in the lobby. A diligent NBC pageboy insisted on calling up to Studio 6B for approval before he let me into an elevator. The corridors on six were quiet as a tomb as I raced to the studio. Inside, Maggie was pacing the room and rubbing her hands together like Lady Macbeth while Rita DeLong sat at a table with nothing on it except a paper sleeve containing an electrical transcription. "It's exactly the way you said it would be," said Rita. She reached for the recording with a tiny white-gloved hand.

"Don't touch it," I shouted. More calmly, I asked, "You didn't touch it, did you? I mean, you didn't touch the surface of the record itself?"

Maggie held up her hands. "We've been performing on a crime program long enough to know about fingerprints, Harry. We both wore gloves." Gingerly, she slipped the large recording from its paper sleeve. "It's just as you said. Recorded only on one side and the only sound on that side is a single gunshot. It comes exactly five minutes from the start. It's just as you said, Harry."

"Where did you find it?"

Rita shifted her eyes toward the control room's darkened window. "Up there. In the storage bins beneath the turntables." Proud of herself, she added, "It was the first place we looked."

"Now that you have it you can prove to the police that David is innocent," Maggie exclaimed.

"Well, it's not quite that simple." She looked crestfallen. "This only shows that maybe Worthington was not killed at five past six. It doesn't prove that David didn't kill him at a later time. He still has no alibi for any of that hour between the end of the dress rehearsal and the moment when he came back to the studio."

Maggie sank to a chair and began to cry. "I thought, I hoped . . ."

"Don't give up, Maggie. This little crime drama isn't over yet. As they say around here, the show's not off the air until the chimes go bong, bong, bong."

A little smile pushed through Maggie's tears. "You're not giving up, then?"

"Hell no. There's more than a little of Detective Fitzroy in me, darling."

"Is there anything we can do?" Rita asked.

"Yes. Put that record back where you found it."

"Put it back?"

"Return it to the exact spot it came from."

"But, Harry," Maggie objected.

"Do this my way, Maggie," I snapped. "I know what I'm doing. Put it back."

"I think you do owe us an explanation," said Rita indignantly.

She was right. They'd done a startling job in finding the disc. I owed them something. "That recording has been there since the murder. The killer knows where he put it and I'm pretty sure he's checked from time to time to make sure it was still there. It's a big thing and he couldn't just walk out with it. He had to leave it. He had to count on its being just another ET among many. In that he obviously felt certain that no one would be looking for that recording. All he had to do was bide his time until it was safe to remove it from its hiding place. If he comes looking for it again and sees it's gone, well . . ."

"Of course you're right, as usual." Rita nodded.

Maggie still looked unconvinced, but I was all she had. "What will you do now?" she asked.

"Let's just say I've got a few things to do and not a lot of time to do them before the cast of *Detective Fitzroy's Casebook* meets in this very studio in a couple of hours to put on the next exciting episode of America's favorite crime show."

## 35

Nobody ever wrote better crime melodramas than Veronica Blake and I doubt if she ever wrote a better one than "The Case of the Black Widow," rehearsed that day in Studio 6B at Radio City. All of the problems of story-line and timing that had kept the cast of *Detective Fitzroy's Casebook* busy all week had been ironed out, and the drama itself proceeded flawlessly while Guff Taylor's recording machines transcribed it for broadcasting that night. When the last thrilling chord from Rita DeLong's organ faded and the ON THE AIR light went off, everyone connected with the show applauded. The show's sponsor clapped me on the back as we watched from the control room and allowed that his commercials and the resulting sales of coffee in grocery stores from coast to coast were not going to suffer at all if everyone continued to give him and the audience shows as fine as this one. J. William Richards was exultant as he charged into the studio to congratulate those who had performed so well. They were basking in his praise when he gave me an anxious glance and announced, "Mr. MacNeil's got a script that he'd like all of you to take a look at and to, uh, run through for me before you all go home." He paused to swallow hard and dab his handkerchief against his perspiring forehead. "I know this is out of the ordinary, but Mr. MacNeil has asked for our cooperation and I've promised it and now I'm asking each of you to give me yours." His tone became a little flinty near the end. The sponsor was speaking. "It won't take long." He turned to me. "You may give them the scripts, Mr. MacNeil."

"Scripts?" Veronica Blake's tone was professionally indignant.

"What is this, MacNeil?" Miles Flannagan sounded like a usurped producer.

"You're kidding," exclaimed Jason Patrick in an incredulous voice that a listener would never hear from Sergeant O'Donnell.

"Damned peculiar," grunted Bart Mason, reaching for his copy of the pages I was handing out. Mason was to play Worthington.

Ben Loman looked bemused. "Do I have a part?" he asked.

"You're the killer," I said, smiling. I made a disappointed face at Sheila Fay. "You're not in it, doll. Sorry."

"May I stay and watch?"

"Miles will be the announcer." He took the script reluctantly.

"Any sound effects?" asked Jerry Nolan.

I handed him a script. "What's radio without sound effects?"

Rita DeLong gazed across the studio from her organ bench. "Musical bridges and mood themes?"

I crossed the room and handed her a copy of the script. "Without music, where's the suspense, eh, Rita?" Finally I gave a copy to Maggie. "And, of course, there are lines for Miss Molloy. It wouldn't be a *Detective Fitzroy's Casebook* without her."

"What's your part, MacNeil?" asked Miles Flannagan sourly.

"Why, I play the detective, of course."

## DETECTIVE FITZROY'S CASEBOOK

"The Case of Murder on Mike"

*Sound effects: In and under. Gunfire, squeal of tires, sirens.*
ANNOUNCER:  Once again the forces of law, order, and justice swing into action as we bring you another exciting story from *Detective Fitzroy's Casebook*, sponsored proudly by Mellow-Gold Coffee, the drink that gets you started and keeps you going . . . the coffee that's never bitter . . . and always better.
*Music: Dramatic sting.*

ANNOUNCER: And now for tonight's thrilling story, I turn you over to Detective Fitzroy . . . with "The Case of Murder on Mike."

*Sound effect: Christmas street sounds (bells, etc.), in and under.*

FITZROY: It was Christmas time in the big town and it looked as if we were going to have a white one, but even in the season of good cheer, murder takes no holiday. [*Sound out*] I was in my office at headquarters when the phone rang.

*Sound effect: Phone rings.*

FITZROY: It was answered by Miss Molloy.

*Sound effect: Phone being picked up.*

MOLLOY: Detective Fitzroy's office. Oh, hi, Sergeant O'Donnell. Sure, he's here. Hold on.

FITZROY: O'Donnell! What's up?

O'DONNELL [*Through a filter*]: I'm over at Radio City, Chief. We've got a homicide on our hands. You'd better get over here.

FITZROY: I'm on the way.

*Sound effect: Police car siren, in full and under, then out.*

FITZROY: I had no way of knowing as I sped uptown in my squad car that we were about to investigate one of the strangest cases in the history of the Homicide Bureau. That day in one of the studios at Radio City [*Fading off*] someone had more than a radio play in mind when . . .

WORTHINGTON [*Fading in*]: Well, what do you want? The person you're looking for is down in the cafeteria with everyone else. Have you noticed that nobody but me seems to care about this radio program? Do I rush out of the studio whenever there's a break and rush to have a cup of coffee and a sandwich? I do not. I stay here in the studio working, perfecting, making things better. So as you see, I am busy, so get out.

KILLER: They all hate you, you know.

WORTHINGTON:  Who hates me?

KILLER:  Everyone connected with the program.

WORTHINGTON:  Humph!

KILLER:  You use people, then throw them away when they're no longer useful to you. Look at the way you've treated David Reed. You led him to believe he would take over the starring role in the program. Then you cut him out on a whim.

WORTHINGTON:  That's my business.

KILLER:  You treat the sponsor with contempt. You give Miles Flannagan the back of your hand. His years of loyalty mean nothing to you. You just cut him out. You treat everyone like dirt—Jason, Veronica, Guff, Jerry, everyone. But worse than any of these is what you've done to Rita.

WORTHINGTON  [*Scornfully*]: Rita?

KILLER:  Yes. I can never forgive you for that. She loved you.

WORTHINGTON:  She's a fool.

KILLER:  She's a fine woman and you're going to pay for what you've done to her.

WORTHINGTON: Pay? Don't make me laugh. What are you going to do about it?

KILLER: I'm going to kill you.

WORTHINGTON: Kill me? [*Laughs*] You're nothing but—

*Sound effect: Gunshot.*

*Music: Dramatic bridge.*

FITZROY:  All right, O'Donnell, what happened here?

O'DONNELL:  We've had a lucky break, Chief. We've got our man.

FITZROY:  Is that so?

O'DONNELL:  The announcer did it. He claims he's innocent, but I'm sure he'll crack under questioning. He's got no alibi for the time of the murder. You see, we know the exact time of the murder because the shot was heard. There's no doubt the announcer did it. No sirree. Here's the way I see it . . .

*Music: Sinister bridge.*

FITZROY: Yep, it looked bad for the announcer, but
something about the whole thing didn't sit well with
me. It was too neat, too easy. So I decided to poke
around a little more. I was certain that someone on
the show killed Worthington. The question was,
how? Everybody had an alibi. So how could someone commit a murder and still have an ironclad alibi?
I was still trying to figure that one out the next day
over a ham and rye and a cup of coffee in the network cafeteria when an old friend walked in.

*Sound effect: Restaurant noises.*

FRIEND: Hello, Fitzroy. How's the crime business?

FITZROY: Not so hot. How's the broadcasting game?

FRIEND: Just swell.

FITZROY: Say, I thought you were on the air at this
hour?

FRIEND [*Laughs*]: I *am* on the air. My program today is
on a transcription. Wonderful things, transcriptions.
I can be on the air at the same time I'm having this
conversation with you, all through the magic of recording.

FITZROY: That's very interesting. Very interesting.

FRIEND: Hey, Fitzroy, where are you going?

FITZROY [*Fading off*]: To find a murderer! To find a murderer!

*Music: Dramatic stab.*

FITZROY: I'd been bothered by the curious fact that a
shot was heard at five after six, but suddenly I saw
how it might have been possible for Worthington to
be killed later than that.

O'DONNELL: Chief, are you asking me to believe that the
shot was a recording?

FITZROY: That's what I'm saying, O'Donnell.

O'DONNELL: But why make a record of a gunshot?

FITZROY: To make us believe something that never happened. To get us to think the wrong way. To mislead

us, Sergeant. We've also been thinking the wrong way about the murderer. We assume one person was involved. But what if the killer had an accomplice?
*Music: Dramatic sting.*
O'DONNELL: That's an interesting theory, Chief, but how are you going to prove it?

# 36

"I didn't have time to write the rest of the script, but it comes to its climax in the scene where the detective has gathered everyone into a room in order to reveal who done it and how, as I have assembled the cast and crew of *Detective Fitzroy's Casebook*. This is also the point at which the detective brings in the police lieutenant who has been investigating the murder. In this case it's Bill Tinney of Homicide." I turned toward the studio door where Tinney had been peering anxiously through the window and waved him in. Close behind him was Ben Turner. "You all remember my friend from the *Daily News*. He was kind enough to recommend me to Maggie Skeffington. I hope you won't mind his sitting in. I promised Ben he'd be the first to know who really killed Derek Worthington. So, if you'll be patient—this will be a little complicated—I'll tell you all how and why the crime was committed."

Veronica Blake applauded. "Nicely done, Harry. The scene is set. It's your cue."

"Thank you. I'll start with the time of the murder. It was assumed from the start that Derek was murdered at five after six. That was when Robby Miller and his tour heard a shot that they thought was a sound effect. Until Derek's body was discovered that was a logical assumption. Then it was found that there was an open mike switch in the control room. Obviously, thanks to that inadvertently opened mike, the fatal shot was heard." I turned toward Guff Taylor. "A technician as good at his job as Guff would not deliberately leave a control room without clearing the board. Is that the right term, Guff?"

"You're a fast learner, Mr. MacNeil," Guff replied with a smart little salute.

"I do my best. Thanks to that mistakenly open mike, the shot had been heard and so the time of the murder was known. It was quickly discerned that everyone connected with the program had an alibi for that time. Everybody except David Reed. The case against Reed looked airtight, but what if Derek had not been murdered at five past six? What if he was killed later than that? What if the shot heard at five after six was not a shot but was truly a sound effect? If that were the case, then maybe no one's alibi would hold up. Eventually that was my very hot theory. But in following it up I discovered that all possible suspects—and I considered all of you suspects—still had unshakable alibis. With the exception of Reed, all of you were able to account for every minute of time between the end of the rehearsal and the moment you all found Derek's body. That brought me back to Reed. If the murder were an inside job, obviously he had to have been the one."

Bill Tinney snorted, "Exactly."

"I was pretty much stuck with that conclusion when something happened to change my whole way of thinking. That sound-effects record that the tour heard at five after six was actually found. Maggie and Rita located it. Theory had turned into fact. If Derek Worthington had *not* been shot at five after six but sometime *later*, that was a very curious thing to me, because now I had to concern myself with that lack of alibi on the part of Reed. If he were going to make a recording of a gunshot, he would have done so in order to give himself an alibi. *Yet he had no alibi.* There was no one to vouch for his whereabouts at five after six. Nor did he have an alibi for the whole hour during which, at some point, Derek was actually murdered. Very curious. With the existence of that record and the lack of a witness to put Reed at the skating rink, my only conclusion had to be that Reed had nothing to do with that recording and therefore had nothing to do with the murder."

Maggie exploded with delight. "Harry, you are wonderful!"

"Thanks, Maggie. It's always nice to be appreciated for one's talents, but I couldn't leave this case at that. Okay, Reed had to be innocent. But someone killed Derek Worthington. The question now was, who pulled that trigger? Logic said it had to be someone from the show. The killer had to have some connection to *Detective Fitzroy's Casebook.* The killer had to know the routines, had to know that Derek would be alone in the studio. Yet all of you remained unshakably accounted for. The cast was in the cafeteria and very visible to cast members of other shows as well as one another. Miles Flannagan and Mr. Richards were in Miles's office. Jerry Nolan was on the air handling the sound effects on another show. Guff Taylor was among his fellow technicians. So who killed Derek and how was it done? How can a person be in two places at the same time?"

"Someone was lying," suggested Ben Turner in a burst of the obvious.

I turned, pointing at Ben. "Very good, Benjamin. Someone was lying."

# 37

The studio was so quiet I could hear the *shush* of the air coming in through the ventilators. It was Veronica Blake who decided to shatter that accusing silence. "You're very good, Harry, to figure that out."

"Coming from the woman who's known as the queen of the crime story, that is a high compliment. However, I was not the only person to realize that someone was lying. A young man named Robby Miller figured it out. The kid apparently had the smarts to grasp what really happened in Studio 6B that night. Unfortunately for him he had the poor judgment to try to cash in on what he knew or suspected. He died because of that. A nasty and dangerous undertaking, blackmail. I can't think of anything riskier for a man to do. Unless it's to scorn a lover. True, Rita?"

I turned to her seated demurely at her studio organ. She blinked at me incredulously, then burst into disdainful laughter. "Are you accusing me of murdering Derek? Because of an affair that was over long ago? Really, Mr. MacNeil, I am disappointed in you. How could I have murdered Derek? I was in the cafeteria. Maggie was with me. Others saw me there; persons from other programs who would have no reason to lie. How could I have killed Derek?"

"You had help."

"Who would be mad enough to help another commit murder?"

"It's been done. In your case, the assistance came from someone who had proved eager to help you provide an alibi for David Reed. I refer to Enrico Avilla. It was Enrico who actually shot Derek."

"That is a lie."

"It is, Rita? We'll see."

"How could Enrico have gotten into Studio 6B?" Veronica Blake was as scornful as Rita. "He's not an employee. You do not get into the studios of Radio City unless you are an employee."

"Not true, Veronica. You can get into Radio City for forty cents. Enrico came in with a guided tour. In fact, he was with the group that Robby Miller was leading. Enrico slipped away from the tour, murdered Derek, and either walked out of Radio City on his own or, and I believe this was more likely, rejoined the tour and left with the crowd. It's easy to slip away from one of those tours. I did it myself. I presume that Robby Miller recognized him and noticed Enrico Avilla's curious behavior. Robby probably knew of Enrico's friendship with Rita. I can only guess. Robby is dead, so he can't tell us what gave him the idea that Rita was involved in the murder of Derek."

"If you are building a case on suppositions regarding the presumed activities of a dead man, you are a fool, Harry," said Rita.

"Oh, I can prove a connection between you and the murder of Robby Miller. You see, when Robby thought his little blackmail scheme was going to pay off he dashed from his hotel and indulged himself in the extravagance of a taxi. I've found the taxi, its driver, and the trip sheet that shows that Robby arrived blissfully unaware that he was heading for his death at number 520 East Fifty-second Street, otherwise known as Wit's End. I'm fairly sure that the doorman at your home will be able to testify that Robby Miller came calling on the night he was murdered."

"Way to go, Harry," exclaimed Ben Turner from the quiet little corner of Studio 6B where he'd been scribbling down notes in a reporter's notebook. "That wraps it up, eh?"

"Not yet, Ben. There's more. A lot more."

# 38

"As skillful as Rita's Latin lover may have been in handling guns, the intricacies of modern radio are, I think, beyond his capabilities, so we still have to explain the existence of that recording of the fake gunshot. We also have to account for how the disc came to be on the turntable in the control room. And how the mike switch happened to be on. Remember, the mike had to be on so that Derek would not hear the shot. Am I correct on that point, Guff?"

The lanky technician nodded.

"And how did the transcription find its way into the storage rack where Rita and Maggie discovered it? These are interesting points that cannot be answered by saying simply that Enrico did all of it. First of all, when the recording was set spinning and when its contents were heard, Enrico was following Robby Miller from the tour mezzanine up to the seventh floor. Clearly, someone else had to put that recording on the turntable and to open the mike switch. Those technical functions could be handled easily by one of the best technicians in radio."

Guff Taylor exploded. "I don't have to stay here and listen to this."

Bill Tinney's penchant for drama surfaced when he showed his policeman's revolver by drawing aside his jacket and patting his holster. "Just stay put, fella."

Veronica Blake scoffed. "This is pure fiction."

"You are certainly the expert on crime stories, Veronica. If anyone can poke a hole in my little tale, it's you."

"Thank you very much."

"Who knows a story better than that story's author?"

"What are you getting at?"

"I'm getting to the scriptwriter of the Radio City murder case. Veronica Blake."

"Good Lord, Harry," cried Veronica, "you're not accusing me of murdering Derek? Me? Murder someone because I felt jilted?"

"The murder of Derek Worthington was not a simple crime of passion. No. This was a carefully plotted murder. It probably had its start in Rita DeLong's smoldering hatred for Derek Worthington. Years of cruelties all came to a head when he announced that he was leaving for California. Leaving! What did that mean for Rita? It meant that all of her lingering hopes that Derek would return to her, beg her for forgiveness, were dashed. Then Rita got the idea to murder Derek, but she knew she would need help. Who did she know who could write a script in which Derek would die and the murderer get away? Radio's finest crime writer."

"Why would I give Rita so much as the time of day if she came to me with a plan to commit murder?"

"Because you had scores to settle with Derek yourself. And you were probably fascinated by the sheer challenge to your mystery writer's mind. The scheme to murder Derek required the kind of brilliant plotting that only someone of your talents could provide, Veronica. And what twists and turns you wrote into the scenario!"

"Quite a plot," she said sarcastically. "A faked gunshot, a mysterious recording that appears and disappears, a swarthy Latin who murders for love. Wow, MacNeil, this is really quite preposterous."

"Ingenious, yes; preposterous, no. It was a script born out of radio. Filled with illusion and trickery with plenty of important parts to be played by superb actors. To carry it off, your script required a remarkable cast. A group of people so close, so attuned to one another, so wrapped up in their work that there's even a name for that kind of acting troupe. It's known as a repertory company. That's what David Reed said the cast of *Detective Fitzroy's Casebook* was and is. Even Derek recognized the cohesiveness of his acting group. It was so important to him that he never fired anyone, with one understandable exception—Freddy Shoemaker. He had plenty of cause to fire David Reed, yet even after Reed slugged him, Derek kept him on. Reed was part of the company. Part of the repertory group."

I paused again, fixing my eyes on Maggie.

Then I said, "What an actor David Reed is! What a brilliant and devoted member of the *Fitzroy* repertory company. He was so dedicated to his fellow actors that he was willing to risk the electric chair."

# 39

"It was a daring and dangerous part Reed had to play. His role was brilliantly conceived and convincingly portrayed. He had to create the charming, vulnerable, and winning youth mistakenly arrested for murder if the plot was to succeed. He undertook the role willingly. Even eagerly, I expect."

Bill Tinney erupted. "What the hell are you saying?"

"If the murderers of Derek Worthington were to get away with their crime, it had to be shown beyond a shadow of a doubt that *no one* on *Fitzroy* could possibly have done it. How to do that? That was the dilemma. It was easy enough to provide one another with alibis, but there was the possibility that it would look too neat. Some cop might smell a rat. So, why not provide the cops with a suspect who did not have an alibi? Why not give the cops a red herring?"

"How in the world could they be sure that Reed wouldn't go to the chair?" It was Ben Turner again, his reporter's pad and pencil poised expectantly before him.

"That, old friend, is where I came in."

Ben nodded slowly and grinned knowingly. "You were to get Reed off."

"And by getting him off, take the heat off the cast and crew of *Detective Fitzroy's Casebook*. If I could produce the recording of the fake gunshot, I would prove that Reed was not the murderer. Why set up that sound effect and not have an alibi? The appearance of the recording made it inescapable that Reed had to be innocent, and since everyone else had those ironclad alibis, I and the cops would have to conclude that an outsider killed Derek Worthington. The repertory group that gave America its most popular crime show would get away with murder and the show would go on. Especially since the sponsor wanted to keep the show on the air. And especially since Miles Flannagan conveniently came up with a piece of paper showing he had inherited the program."

Flannagan roared, "Are you trying to implicate me, sir?"

"Ah, you ask how could you be involved when you and Mr. Richards were in your office? Well, we have only the word of the two of you on that. I'd be willing to accept your word if I didn't have to come back to that transcription with that single gunshot sound effect on it. You see, I was nagged by the problem of how that ET got off the turntable and into the storage rack. It was vital that it be out of sight by the time Derek's body was discovered. Murder draws crowds and it wouldn't do to have that incriminating ET lying out in the open. I first supposed that Guff Taylor might have removed it, but Guff always came back to the control room just before air time. That was his routine and he couldn't change the routine on the night that Derek Worthington was going to be found dead. So who took that ET and stuck it out of sight? Who else was in that control room that night? J. William Richards was there."

The sponsor howled. "You will hear from my attorneys to answer for that slander, Mr. MacNeil."

"I think your lawyers will have more important matters to take care of, sir. Your defense in a case of murder."

"Outrageous!"

Bill Tinney looked more than a little bewildered and sounded it. "Harry, are you insinuating they all had a part in this?"

"In a repertory company, each has a part, no matter how small. Each plays a role. And there are those whose assigned chores are offstage. In this case, off the air."

I crossed the studio to the sound-effects truck.

"This drama could not have been put on at all without a superb sound-effects man."

"Jerry Nolan and Guff Taylor collaborated on the recording of the fake gunshot on the ET," I continued. "Before leaving the control room at the end of the rehearsal, Guff dead-rolled the ET so that it would play that gunshot at five after six. He opened the mike switch so Derek wouldn't hear the shot. All easily done. But neither Jerry nor Guff could dispose of the ET later on. As I've said, Mr. Richards got that part. It must have been a thrill for such a radio buff to actually handle real broadcast equipment, even if it was just a recording. That disc was crucial and so I became suspicious when it turned up the way it did just in time to get me not to give up on this case. I found it interesting that the discovery of the recording was made by Rita DeLong. It was Rita who earlier came up with a pitiful attempt to provide Reed with an alibi in the person of Enrico Avilla. At the time I put that down as a touching but inept gesture by a woman as sentimental as her music. When Rita found that recording, I had to look at Rita in a different way."

The studio fell deathly still again except for the *shush* of the ventilators. This time I broke the silence.

"At this point I decided to take a look at this whole case from a new angle, discounting no one as a suspect no matter what he had for an alibi."

Maggie Skeffington was ashen. Slowly shaking her head, her Miss Molloy voice unaccustomedly trembly, she muttered, "Harry, how can you possibly believe that Rita, Miles, Jerry—all of them—could do this?"

"It's the only explanation, Maggie."

"When I came to you I never thought that—"

"No, you never thought. You never dreamed I'd be able to prove that you and your friends were up to your necks in a conspiracy to murder. You expected that I'd see all of you as innocents caught in a terrible web of circumstances. You thought I'd be so charmed by your performances that I'd never see the truth behind the fiction you all created so convincingly. You, Maggie, were the best. You had the hardest part of all. You had the role of making a sucker out of me. You had to get me to play my part perfectly because if you didn't, then your boyfriend stood a real chance of going to the electric chair. You're a great actress, Maggie. Right from the start you had me twisted around your little finger and you knew it. You knew I could be counted on to be just good enough to get David Reed out of jail but not good enough to figure out what happened. But just in case I started getting out of control, in case I started ad-libbing my part, you and Veronica were ready to play your parts to the hilt once more to direct my attentions elsewhere and to protect your friends. Veronica's part was to keep me to the script, but murder in life isn't at all like murder on the radio. In life no one has the luxury of rewriting when the play isn't working out right."

Maggie was crying real tears. No acting this time.

"I assume it was Veronica who thought up the part for a private eye. It was pure genius. Casting Maggie to be the one to bring a private eye into the case was truly inspired. What guy could see that angelic face and not believe every word she said?" I winked at her. "I couldn't. Not at first."

Maggie turned away and sank into a chair sobbing.

"The idea was to provide the private eye with just enough bits and pieces to keep him interested and convinced that Reed was a poor innocent victim. Maggie's love and trust would go far on that point. Of course, there was risk. God, what a risky enterprise all this was! There was the possibility that the detective Maggie hired wouldn't be good enough to follow the clues he was to be provided. At that point a new one could be gotten, I suppose, but lucky, plucky Maggie found me right at the start. Good old sentimental Harry MacNeil, a pushover for a sweet face. That I was an ex-cop was icing on the cake; lots of friends in the police department and the D.A.'s office. Maggie's part was to find a private eye who would be just smart enough to get Reed off but not *too* smart, and apparently Maggie decided I filled the bill."

Rita DeLong shouted, "This is nothing but guesswork. You have no proof."

"I have Enrico Avilla. Rather, Lieutenant Tinney has him. The police are at your apartment right now, Rita, and I expect they they'll find Enrico there. With luck they'll find the gun he used to kill Robby Miller. Must have been no problem at all for Enrico to get Robby's body out of your apartment and into the river. The water's practically below your windows. I'm sure we can persuade Enrico that there's nothing to be gained by denying his part in the murders. He's obviously devoted to you, Rita. It took real devotion to risk a perjury charge by sticking to that phony alibi you dreamed up for Reed. I figured a man who'd do that was either a fool or head over heels in love."

"Same thing," muttered Ben Turner from his corner of the studio.

There was nothing left to do at that point except let the police take over.

Maggie was the last one out the studio door with one of Bill Tinney's homicide detectives escorting her. She paused a moment before leaving and turned to look at me with tears sparkling at the corners of her eyes. She was a scared girl from a little hick town in Pennsylvania, but only for an instant. Then she squared her shoulders, stuck out her chin, and gave me a snappy little salute. "See you around, MacNeil."

The voice—ah, the voice!

It belonged to Miss Molloy.

No question about that. No sirree.

Assistant D.A. Timothy Brogan didn't mind at all that his plans for a cozy Christmas around the tree with wife and kiddies had been knocked into a cocked hat by the need to wrap up the Worthington murder as neatly as a bundle of joy from Santa Claus. There was a twinkle in his eyes that would have done credit to old Saint Nick himself as he poured Scotch for himself and me in his office high above the holiday stillness of the streets of lower Manhattan. "I've got a platoon of people taking down statements. The whole story is coming out and it's pretty much the way you figured it, Harry. That dreamy Latin lover who was the actual tiggerman understands that the only way to keep himself out of the hot seat is to turn state's witness, so he's singing his heart out. He's admitted shooting Worthington and the Miller kid. Yeah, the kid tried to shake him down. A very sharp-eyed kid, he was. The way Enrico tells it, Miller had noticed Enrico around Radio City a couple of times before he took the tour on the night Worthington was killed. The kid spotted that Enrico slipped away for a while on that particular tour, and later when Worthington was found dead, the kid put two and two together. He decided what he saw would add up to a handsome payoff in blackmail. Rita DeLong was willing to pay."

"But Enrico suggested the alternative?"

"So she says. Enrico says otherwise. Doesn't matter, really, does it?"

"I guess not."

"They'll all face murder charges. One guy may pull the trigger, but when he does it with the help of others, they're just as guilty in the eyes of the law. They'll all do time. Maybe none will get the chair, what with the bargaining that's going on to get them to sign confessions." He sipped a little more Scotch, then shook his head. "What a bunch of saps they were to think they could get away with it." He glanced at me slyly and smiled. "They were nuts to think they could put something over on you, Harry."

"They almost did. *She* almost did."

Brogan stared up at the ceiling for a moment and I knew he was thinking about the same person who was on my mind. "Those are the dangerous ones, Harry. The ones with the sweet faces. The colleens. The Maggie Skeffingtons."

They kept *Detective Fitzroy's Casebook* on the air. Of course, there was a new cast of actors in the parts and they were pretty good, but I only listened to the program once after that. For me it just wasn't the same. Not without Maggie.

# About the Author

H. Paul Jeffers spent his boyhood listening to crime programs on the radio but now divides his time between writing novels and running the news department of WCBS Radio in New York City.